No part of this publication may be reproduced, stored in a retrieval system, or transmitted in any form or by any means, electronic, mechanical, photocopying, recording, scanning, or otherwise, without the prior written permission of the publisher, except in the case of brief quotations within critical reviews and otherwise as permitted by copyright law.

NOTE: This is a work of fiction. Names, characters, places, and incidents are a product of the author's imagination. Any resemblance to real life is purely coincidental. All characters in this story are 18 or older.

Copyright © 2020, Willow Winters Publishing. All rights reserved.

Evan
&
Kat

Willow Winters
WALL STREET JOURNAL & USA TODAY BESTSELLING AUTHOR

Book 1 in the seductive duet for Evan and Kat, from Wall Street Journal Bestselling Author, Willow Winters. A high heat and high emotion romance in the tempting and wealthy elite social circles in New York... and all the corruption that comes with it.

I married the bad boy from Brooklyn.
The one with the tattoos and the look in his eyes that told me he was bad news.
The look that comes with all sorts of warnings.

I knew what I was doing.
I knew by the way he put his hands on me; how he owned me with his forceful touch.
I couldn't say no to him, not that I wanted to. That was then, and it seems like forever ago.

Years later, I've grown up and moved on. But he's still the man I married. Dangerous in ways I don't like to think about. I did this to myself. I knew better than to fall for him.

I only wish love was enough to fix this...

You Know I Love You is book 1 of a duet. It is the second duet in the series, but it can be read first.

Prologue

Kat

It only took one night; one moment, and my fate was sealed. He knew I would never tell him no.

I wonder what would have happened if I'd never met Evan. The thought makes my stomach sink and twist, and a cold chill flows in waves over my body.

It *pains* me to consider such a thing. To have never been with the man I love.

Dragging in a lungful of cold air, I steady myself with deep breaths.

It physically hurts to imagine not having him in my life for the last six years.

I didn't know I was setting myself up for heartbreak all

those years ago. Yet here I am, and that reality is what keeps me up at night. My eyes burn from both exhaustion and the tears begging to be shed.

That chance encounter set everything into motion, and only months ago I would have said it was a blessing, bestowed upon me by fate, or maybe kismet. But now I know better.

I wish I'd never stopped that night.

I wish I'd never met Evan at that gas station.

Whoever said it's better to have loved and lost than never to have loved at all was a liar and a fool.

This pain isn't worth it.

If only I could go back, because I don't know how we'll get through this.

Chapter 1

Kat

Tell me a lie and make it sweet,Like the vows you made on
our wedding day.
Tell me a lie, don't make it hurt,
The pain in my chest won't go away.
Don't tell me the truth, I can't face what's to come.
I'll yell and I'll kick, I'll fight it, I'll run.
Don't tell me the truth, I don't want to hear.
Tell me pretty lies with whispers sincere.

The chill on my skin lingers and flows down my shoulders. It's an odd sensation that travels across my arms and I'd like to blame it on the alcohol, but I've felt it all day. From the very start of this morning, before the drinks came easier and easier. For days, really, I've been feeling this strange sensation of not quite being in my own body. As if I'm not really here. This isn't really happening to me.

It's been going on for more than a few days if I'm honest ... maybe even weeks, but I've been ignoring the signs and whispers, pretending like they weren't real.

Now that this sickness won't leave me, I can't deny it.

Ever since I let the words slip through my lips.

I hate you.

You're a fucking liar.

I want a divorce.

An ache in my chest prompts me to take a sip of wine. Letting it slide down my throat, I pretend that it soothes me. It's numbing, that's what it is. That's what I need. Tears prick at my eyes, but I don't let them fall. Instead a shuddering breath leaves me and I lift up my glass, downing the remaining wine. It's too sweet for being so dark.

Startled by a sound from the floor above me, the glass nearly tips over as I set it down quickly to wipe under my eyes. I don't want him to see me cry; I won't let him. But the creak I heard was a false alarm. I don't hear the heavy footsteps of him coming down the stairs to our townhouse. I'm still alone in the dining room, waiting for him to leave.

Left only with bittersweet memories and the constant question: *How did this happen?*

The thick, dark drapes behind me are pulled shut but even they can't completely drown out the night sounds of busy New York City. There's always a bit that travels through. It used to bother me when I initially moved here, but now it's soothing. It calms me as my gaze drifts toward the empty stairwell, where it lingers.

I shouldn't be drunk, not when I'm supposed to be preparing to meet with a potential client tomorrow. As one of the top literary agents in New York City, I'm damn good at what I do but tonight, I don't care.

I shouldn't have closed my laptop and logged off all social media when I have promotions and advertisements running around the clock for these launches.

I shouldn't be doing a lot of things.

But here I am, sitting at the head of the dining room table, and I refuse to do anything but watch the stairs and wait for him to leave. The very thought of staring at his back as the front door closes forces me to reach for the bottle.

I listen carefully as I pour the last of the wine into my glass. He's packing at the last minute, like he always does, but this time it's so much different. He's traveling for work, but when he leaves from his rendezvous in London, he's not coming back here. That sudden realization brings a fresh flood of unshed tears to burn my eyes, but I remain very still. As if maybe playing dead will hold back these emotions.

"He better not," I mutter beneath my breath, holding on to my resolve.

I lift the glass to my lips, the dark cabernet tasting sweeter and sweeter with each sip, lulling me into a lethargy where the memory of yesterday fades.

Where the article doesn't exist. Where the denial of an affair can fall on deaf ears. The picture itself was innocent. But Evan doesn't have a single explanation for me. He can't make clear to me why he's lying, why he's stumbling over his words to come up with a justification.

What hurts the most is the look in his eyes when he lies to me. The paparazzi photo is of him with his boss's wife Samantha, who just so happens to be in the middle of a vicious divorce. He was with her at 3:00 in the morning in her hotel lobby. Three fucking a.m. *Nothing good happens past 2:00 a.m.* He used to make that joke all the time when we first met. I used to laugh with him when he said it.

There's only one explanation for that photograph and both of us know it. Even though he can't come up with a plausible excuse, he still denies it. It's a slap in my face. I'm done pretending like I can forgive him for this. If he can't give me his truth, I'm left with my own, which is that my husband is not the man I fell in love with. Or at the very least, his decisions aren't ones I can live with.

I suck in a long, deep breath, pushing my phone away as it beeps again with a message from a friend and I lean back in my chair. I don't want to read it. With the palms of my hands, I cover my eyes, suddenly feeling hot. Too hot.

They keep asking me the same things, but with different

words.

Maddie: *Are you all right?*

Julia: *Is it true? It can't be true.*

Suzette: *So you went through with it? Is there anything I can do?*

Messages from my friends have been hitting my phone one by one, each of them making it vibrate on the table throughout the day.

It takes everything in me to face them, as if they were really here in person asking me all these questions. I don't have answers to give them, none that I want to say out loud anyway. I'm not pushing away my husband because I want to. I'm doing it because I have to and I don't have the resolve to speak that confession.

Even I'm disappointed in myself.

My friends want what's best for me. They only want to help me and I know that's the truth, but it doesn't keep me from being angry at the phone as it goes off again.

Heaving in a deep breath, I wish I wasn't in the big city. I wish I wasn't well known. I wish I could hide under the guise of anonymity and just be no one. More importantly, I wish no one knew. I'd crawl back to him if that were the case. I'd beg him to hold me every time I cried, even if he's the one who brought out this side of me.

I'd beg him to love me. He would, I know it. And then I'd hate myself.

You deserve better than this. Another message from Suzette comes through next and I can only run the pad of my thumb down the screen over her words. It's an attempt to make myself believe it.

Just leave me alone. Everyone get out of my life, my marriage. It wasn't for them to see. It's not for them to judge like every fucking gossip column in New York City. It's not the first time our marriage has been mentioned in the papers, but I pray it'll be the last.

My knuckles turn white as I grip the phone with the intent of throwing it, letting it smack against the wall to silence it, but I don't. It's the sound of Evan's boots rhythmically hitting each step as he walks down the stairs that forces me to compose myself. At the very least I pretend to; he's always seen through it, though. He knows how much this kills me.

I hit the button to turn off my phone and ignore the texts and calls, squaring my shoulders as I attempt to pull myself together.

I haven't answered a single message or email since this morning when Page Six came out with an article about our separation. It's funny how I only uttered the words two nights ago, yet it was already circulating gossip columns before the weekend hit, blasted all over social media. I wonder if he wanted this. If that was Evan's way of finally pushing his workaholic wife to the brink of divorce.

My gaze morphs into a glare as he comes into view, but it

doesn't stay long. My skin is suddenly feeling hotter, but in a way that's joined with desire. I can't help but to imagine how his rough stubble would feel against my palm as I caressed his cheek, how his lips would taste as he leaned down to kiss me. A very large part of me wants to savor it. Our last goodbye kiss. It's funny how the goodbye kisses are the ones I value most, but I won't let him kiss me before he leaves this time. Not when the last things that came from his lips were lies.

My deep inhales are silent, although the heavy rise and fall of my chest betrays me. If he notices, he doesn't let on as he places his luggage by the front door. My own hands turn numb watching his.

Even if he is only wearing a pair of faded jeans and a plain white T-shirt, he's still devilishly handsome. It's his muscular physique and tanned, tattooed skin that let you know he's a classic bad boy regardless of what he's wearing. My heart beats slower as the seconds pass between us; it's calming just to look at him. That's how he got me in the beginning. The desire and attraction are undeniable despite what he's done.

He's the first to break our gaze as he runs his fingers through his dark brown hair and lets out an uneasy sigh. In response my lips curl into a sarcastic smile, mocking both me and my thoughts. I'm not the only one to fall for his charm and allure, but I should have learned my lesson by now. My fingers slip down the thin stem of the wineglass as I smile weakly and force back the sting in my eyes, pretending I'm not going to cry, pretending that I've made my decision final. Like I don't already regret it.

"I have to go," Evan states after a moment of uncomfortable silence, apart from the constant background hum of traffic.

My blood rushes and I try to swallow the lump in my throat. I focus on the wine, the dark red liquid pooling in the base of the glass. I try to swirl it, but it doesn't move; there's so little left.

"Is she going to be there?" I ask him, staring straight ahead at a black and white photo of the two of us taken years ago on vacation in Mexico.

Why? Why even bother? Why did I let it slip out? I'd planned to just say goodbye. Just end this suffering already.

As he answers, I continue to stare at the genuine smile on my face and then to where his arm is wrapped possessively around my waist in the photograph.

I hate that I asked. It's my insecurity, my hate. My envy even.

"No, she's not. And I already told you it doesn't matter." Any trace of a smile or even of disinterest leaves me. I can't hide what it does to me, what his lie has done to me.

It doesn't matter. Let it go. They're all non-answers. They're words to hide the truth and we both know it.

My elbow is planted on the table as I rest my chin in my hand and try to cover up how much it hurts. To keep it from him just like he's keeping the truth from me, even if I sniff a little too loud. I speak low as I stare straight ahead at nothing in particular. "You told me it's not true, but you didn't deny it to the press," I tell him and finally look him in the eye. "You didn't deny it to anyone but me, and I know you're lying." My words crack at the end and I have to tear my gaze away. "It's been different since you came home." My last statement is drawn out and practically a whisper. It's been difficult between us over the past year, but the last two weeks ... The tension between us changed the second he came home. I knew something bad had happened. I knew it.

Everyone told me to be careful and warned me about Evan six years ago when I first started seeing him. I knew what I was doing when I first said yes to a date with him, when I gave myself to him and let myself fall for someone like him. I'm a fool.

"I told you, Kat, it's not what it looks like," he says and his voice is soft, like he's afraid to say the words louder.

"Then why not tell them?" I ask, staring into his pleading expression. "Why let the world believe you've cheated on me? What could you possibly gain?" Each question gets louder as the words rush out of my mouth. I'm ashamed of how much passion there is in my voice. How much of my pain is on display.

In stark contrast is how little pain he shows and I don't miss how he hasn't budged. He hasn't made a single move to come to me. So I stay planted in my seat as well.

I know why he doesn't deny it, and it's because it's true. Years of just the two of us have shown me who he is and I know he's not a liar, but he's lying to me now. I've never been more sure of anything in my life. "It's been weeks, hasn't it?" I say, forcing out the words from between clenched teeth. This morning I couldn't talk without screaming. Without slamming my fists onto the table, making it shake and causing a glass of water to fall and shatter on the hardwood floor.

I reached my breaking point when he looked me in the eye and told me there was nothing to that picture. I refuse to listen when he lies; not when he does such a horrible job of it.

"Stop it, Kat," Evan commands firmly and his voice is harsh and unforgiving, like I'm the one in the wrong.

"Oh, I see," I respond, raising a brow and feeling a sick smile tug at my lips. "You can cheat, you can lie, but I should be quiet and give you a kiss on the way out to go do whatever you want to do?"

"Don't do this," he says with a rawness that makes my heart clench.

"Then tell me what happened. I know something did." He's been distant, even cold toward me ever since he came home.

A moment passes and I lose my composure again, bared to him in every way as I wait for an answer. But I don't get the one thing I need. The truth. *Or a believable lie.*

"I have to go," is all he says as he gathers his luggage. Slinging a black duffle bag over one shoulder, gripping a suitcase with his other hand, he adds, "I love you."

He says the words without looking at me.

I love you.

It hurts so damn much because he knows I love him. He knows it and he throws the words back at me like it doesn't matter that he's risking it all.

"If you won't tell me the truth," I say lowly as I stare at the table, pushing out the words and feeling each one slice open the cut in my heart that much deeper, "then don't bother coming back." My throat tightens and my lungs refuse to fill as silence is all that answers me.

There's only a slight hesitation, a small creaking sound as he adjusts his grip on the luggage. That's all I get. That's it. The creak of the floorboards that's barely heard over my racing heart.

He leaves without attempting to kiss me or approaching me in the least. His strides don't break in cadence until the heavy walnut front door opens and closes, leaving me with nothing but the tortured sob that's desperate to come up and the faint sounds of the city life filling the empty space once again.

My hands tremble as I close my eyes and try to calm down.

If he really loved me, he wouldn't have let it come to this.

If he loved me, he'd tell me the truth.

Secrets break up marriages.

I keep telling myself that he's to blame, but as a cry rips up my throat and I bring my knees into my chest, my heels resting on the seat of the chair, I replay the last few years and I know I'm at fault too. Deep down, I know. I bury my face in my knees and rock slightly, feeling pathetic as I break down yet again.

If I were him, I'd have cheated on me too.

He says he didn't. He swears it's a lie.

But he doesn't explain it. He can't even look me in the eye.

I did this to myself. I should've known better.

Chapter 2

Evan

When did I turn into the piece of shit I am right now?

Pathetic. That's how I feel as the plane rumbles beneath my feet and I shake my head slightly, waving off the flight attendant and whatever small bag of snacks she was offering.

I crack my neck to the left and right as a ding indicates the seatbelt sign is off and everyone can move about the cabin. I have no intention of getting up or doing a damn thing other than sit here and try to figure out exactly where it all went wrong.

The Wi-Fi is available and I take my time setting it up, prolonging the moment when I'll have to face the fact that she most likely hasn't messaged me. She can yell at me, hit me, take it all out on me, but her silence is what kills me. Her shutting me out is like a knife to the heart.

There's no way to make it right, but I'm not letting her go.

Kat's mine. My wife. *My love.* She's everything to me, even if she hates me to the point where I'm nothing to her.

We used to be ... Something special. Something other assholes dream about and pray for. And now? I couldn't even kiss her before leaving. The very thought of doing it felt too much like goodbye. Like the kind of goodbye that would kill me.

She's kidding herself if she thinks I'm not coming home to her. I don't care that we're going through this, I don't care how bad our fighting is or that I fucked up beyond repair. She doesn't know what happened and I hope she never will, but that doesn't change the fact that she's mine. Above all else, I love her and she loves me. She can't deny that.

My seat groans as I readjust in first class. I clear my throat and clench my teeth as the plane rumbles again, reminding me that she's miles and miles away. Reminding me that I left her again.

I can't bring myself to feel like I deserve her forgiveness. Or that I deserve her at all. That's always been the case between us. She's always been too good for me. The guilt is all-consuming and now I'm trapped in a corner, desperately looking for a way out of the mess I've gotten myself into.

My computer pings as the plane continues to fly across the ocean taking me farther away from her, and I lean forward to check it. I'm far too quick to do it too, praying it's Kat.

Praying's never helped me before and sure enough, it didn't this time either. It's only a message from James, my boss and Samantha's now ex.

My teeth grind against one another, making my jaw even more tense as I read the message. It's the schedule for the rest of the day and my room number for the hotel.

It feels like a slap in the face. I can't keep up this façade and live each day as if nothing's happened. Pretending like nothing's changed.

The back of my head pushes into the seat as I take a calming breath.

Stuck between a rock and a hard place is an inadequate saying.

I'm fucked. Just waiting for them to pick, pick, pick away at me while I have my hands tied behind my back.

Only years ago, I loved my life. It was a high most would be envious of. This is what I wanted more than anything. On the outside, it's glamorous. I stay at five-star resorts, party with celebrities and have every sinful pleasure at my fingertips. That's what a life of helping the rich and famous avoid prison has afforded me.

I protect the clients from any bad press, keep charges from sticking, and avoid any altercations that could lead to something ... unwanted. In return, I'm paid generously and live the high life.

I didn't sign up for *this*, but I sure as fuck cashed every check along the way. My email beeps and it's another message from James, as if confirming that exact thought: this is exactly what I signed up for. It's what I asked for.

Let me know when you land. That's all the email says.

I clear my throat as my hand clenches into a fist and I run the rough pad of my thumb over my knuckles slowly. My reflection in the screen stares back at me and I note the scowl, the dark circles under my eyes. *The anger.*

When I was younger, this was all I wanted. I get paid to party and live in a perpetual state of drunkenness. I lived for the thrill.

Kat used to love it too. Years ago, when we first met and things were different. I glance at the empty seat to my left and picture her sitting beside me. She used to play with the buckle on every flight. Unbuckle, buckle, unbuckle, buckle. At first I thought it was a nervous habit that had to do with a fear of flying, but it was just due to the excitement.

She loved coming with me to events. It was what we did together. Back when everything was the way it was supposed to be.

Back when life was less complicated.

Back when we were kids and I didn't realize that life was going to catch up to me and her career was going to take off, placing us on two very different paths in life.

A huff of a sigh leaves me as I shift in my seat and look back to my computer.

I click over to the flight tab and see there are four hours remaining until we land in London. Four hours to sit in silence and dwell on each and every moment where I fucked up. Every step I took that led me to this very hour.

I turned thirty-two just four months ago, but I'm living the same life I had when we were in our twenties.

She's the one who changed.

She grew up and I'm the one who screwed up.

I run a hand down my face, trying to get the images out of my head.

She can never know, but I was a fool to think I'd hidden it from her.

There's no way out of this.

How can she love me when she knows I'm lying to her?

How can she forgive me for a sin she has no idea I've committed?

How can I keep her when I don't deserve her?

Chapter 3

Kat

"So this is all bullshit?" Sue asks with a tone that says she believes otherwise as she motions to the newspaper. Her voice is soft, but my nerves make it seem louder than it is here in this small coffee shop. I almost shush her before realizing she's not speaking loudly at all.

"It doesn't look like it's …" I can't finish my thought, my eyes drawn to the same picture I stared at for hours last night, plus the night before.

"Well, she's all over him. There's no denying that."

"Women are always all over him." My answer comes out flat. I'm nothing if not blunt and transparent. It's one of the reasons my clients trust me.

"I used to like it ... when they'd try to be all over him," I admit to her but bite my tongue at the urge to voice the additional confession: *I loved it.* "How they'd fawn over him, desperate for Evan's attention. But he only had eyes for me."

"Why is this one any different then?" The paper hits the slick surface of the coffee table as she tosses it down and immediately digs into her large Chanel hobo bag. I know she believes exactly what Evan denied. It's written all over her perfectly red, pursed lips. This is only an attempt to appease me.

It's not the first, the second, or even the third time Evan's had his name in the tabloids for less than angelic reasons. Suzette has her opinions, but she's always refrained from voicing them when it comes to Evan.

His reputation and his livelihood depend on the fact that he's gotten away with things that would send most people to jail for the night.

That was the case before I met him, anyway. Now he gets paid to make sure his clients meet the same fate.

Sue talks as she pulls out a tube of deep red lipstick and a compact mirror. "Do you think he really did it this time?" she asks as if the weight of our marriage doesn't rest on my answer.

The reason this time is different is because I know there's truth to it.

It's because of how he reacts.

It's how he looks at me as if he's guilty.

"He says it's not what it looks like," I answer and roll my

eyes as I do, trying to downplay the pain that coils in my chest. My throat goes tight, but I'm saved by the return of Maddie.

For so many years, since I first moved here really, there's been one constant. It's these women. Jules, my first client and the New York socialite who brought us all together, isn't here. I owe her so much for helping my career take off as quickly as it did, but Jules has everything and all she really wants is companionship. She's getting settled into married life, but she'd be here if I asked. Maddie and Sue were both available and to be honest, I'd prefer them right now. They're not helplessly in love and therefore blind as a bat.

"Pumpkin spice," Maddie says as she sets a hot cup of coffee down in front of me. She doesn't look me in the eyes, like she's afraid doing even that will make me cry.

The strong scent of cinnamon smacks me in the face, but I wrap my hand around the cup, giving her a grateful smile as she takes her seat to my right. I don't like flavored coffee—I don't even like pumpkin, but I'll drink it. I desperately need the caffeine.

My gaze travels to Sue, sitting straight across from me as she returns to the conversation and says, "He says it's not what it looks like?" Her brow quirks as she adds, "... And what does that mean?" It's not a question, it's an accusation and the two of us know it.

"What does what mean?" Maddie asks innocently, the legs of her chair scraping along the floor.

"It means he's lying," Sue answers matter-of-factly and folds the newspaper over, reading the article again. It's only a paragraph, maybe two. It doesn't say much other than the fact that Samantha Lapour and her husband James are now separated, due to an affair she had with my husband, Evan Thompson. Which is a blatant lie. Their marriage has been on the rocks for months and they were separated long before this happened.

Inwardly I cringe at defending my husband at all. An affair is an affair. In an effort to ease the guilt that weighs down my chest, I rub the small spot just below my collarbone.

Maddie's expression turns hard with a look of warning that would normally make me laugh considering how petite and naïve she is. "We're talking about Evan," she says under her breath. Her eyes stay on Sue, who slowly purses her lips and acknowledges Maddie with only a short nod.

The newly divorced Suzette doesn't give men a chance to explain. For good reason, seeing as how she's been through hell and back.

"I'm sorry," Maddie whispers and then clings to her own coffee. French vanilla if I had to guess.

"It's fine," I say lowly, shaking off the emotions rocking through my body and easing the tension at the table. "There's no reason for us to get into this." I don't look at either of them, blowing on the hot coffee and reluctantly drinking it. I don't taste it on the way down, though.

"Well, what do you think?" Maddie asks me and then she puts down her own cup. The coffee shop on Madison Avenue is fairly empty, probably due to the rain and chill of the late fall in the air.

As the shop door opens with a small chime and the busy sounds of the street flood into the small space for a moment, I think of how to answer her.

I don't know what to say.

I think he cheated on me.

I think he's sorry and he regrets it.

I think he loves me. No, I know he loves me.

And I feel like a fool for still loving him and wanting him.

That's what's in my head as I look around the small coffee shop, taking in every detail of the bright white chair rail and cream walls. The framed macro photographs of coffee pots and coffee beans keep my attention a little longer. I've never really noticed them before. This place is so familiar, yet I couldn't have described any of these details if someone had asked me. I've been coming here for years and yet I'd never cared enough to look at what was right here in front of me.

"Why would he lie to you?" Maddie asks, pulling my attention back to her. She huffs, sitting back and causing the chair to grind against the floor as she does. "I just can't imagine Evan doing this." My shoulders rise with a deep intake of breath as I pick at a small square napkin on the table.

I roll the tiny piece I've ripped off between my forefinger

and thumb, watching as it crumples into a small ball.

"I don't know why," I answer softly. I can feel all the overwhelming sadness and betrayal rise up and make my throat tighten as I try to come up with a response. "Maybe I'm stupid, but I can't remember him ever lying to me before." I swallow thickly and flick the tiny ball onto the table. "Not like this." Defeat drips from my words.

"Sorry," I tell them and wipe under my tired eyes, hating that I could possibly feel the telltale prick of tears behind them given how much I've already cried. "I tried not to let it ..." I can't finish. I watch as the rain batters the large glass window in the front of the shop and I slip my internal armor back on.

"Don't you dare be sorry," Sue says with a strength that pulls my attention back to her. Her jet-black hair cut into a blunt bob sways as she leans forward, moving closer to me while she speaks with an undeniable authority. "If you want to cry, cry. If you want to scream, do it. Whatever you need to do, just let it out."

Maddie nods her head in my periphery, but I can't do the same. Looking at the two of them, the stark contrast between Maddie and Suzette is more than obvious. Maddie's a young brunette with large doe eyes, equally in love with love itself and the big city. Sue's a recent divorcée with a bitter sense of humor she's earned. Even their fashion choices are at odds. Maddie's wearing a maxi dress and has a teal raincoat and clear umbrella hanging off the back of her chair, while Sue's in a black and white tweed dress with a matching jacket, plus a broad-brimmed, black Breton hat she wears to keep people away.

Somewhere in the middle is where I fall.

What if I want to deal with it by falling into his arms and letting him lie to me? I bite my tongue, letting the silence be eaten up by the ticking of the clock. I know it's not okay, yet that's all I want. I want him to fight for me. I want him to love me. I want to forgive him, even if he won't admit what he's done.

And that makes me a coward and a pathetic excuse for a modern-day woman, doesn't it?

The snide thought makes me turn my attention back to the dreary state of affairs outside. The clouds have set in and the sky quickly turns dark.

"This is crap weather for a first meeting," I say out loud, not really meaning to.

"Way to change the topic," Sue half jokes as she picks up her coffee cup and takes a sip, the smirk ever present on her lips. Her light blue eyes stare back at me from over the rim and it almost makes me laugh. Almost.

"So you're meeting your client here?" Maddie asks, gracefully accepting my invitation to talk about anything else. I've never loved her more than in this very moment.

I nod, still not trusting myself to speak and take another gulp of my coffee. I forgot it was pumpkin spice and I nearly spit it out, startled by the flavor, but then I swallow it down. It's not so bad.

Maddie pulls her dark brown, curly hair over her shoulder and scrunches her nose as she takes in my expression. "You don't like pumpkin?" she asks, raising a brow in disbelief.

"It's okay," I say, answering her with a straight face and Sue erupts with a laugh that catches the attention of an elderly couple behind us. Her good humor is infectious and I find myself smiling. This is what I need. To talk and think about something else. Anything else.

"I'll get you something else," Maddie says as Sue starts to speak. "Just regular? Cream and sugar?"

"Thanks, but don't worry about it, Maddie. It's good." I wave off her concern and take another sip. "I just needed some caffeine."

"Well, you look professional," Sue says with a nod. "The rain didn't ruin your hair."

I shake out my hair playfully in response to Sue's attempt at a distraction but Maddie doesn't pick up on the hint, and when I yawn, she goes right back to the conversation I hoped we were done with.

"Trouble sleeping?" Maddie asks and I nod my head once then turn back to the cup, hating that we're back on this again.

"I just wish I had ..." I can't finish the sentence and I struggle to come up with something to say as I push the hair from my face while trying to remember what I want. I haven't got a clue. "I wish I had my life together," I practically whisper, but they hear and I know they do.

"You do have your life together. You're an established publisher. An entrepreneur and a hard worker."

I have work. Yes. Maddie happily agrees with Sue, reminding me of how many people in this very city would kill for my job.

But I don't have a damn thing else. Not enough to hold on to a life I somehow strayed from.

The thought makes me miserable and I focus on the coffee again, knocking it back as if it'll save me. When I set it down, I notice how empty it is as I tap the bottom of it against the table and hear a hollow sound. I'm going to need a refill. I'll get it myself, though. I push away from the table slightly. "I'm going to grab another. At this rate it'll be empty before Jacob gets here."

"Oh, Jacob." Sue says his name with a hint of something I can't describe in her voice. A devilish smile grows on her face and it makes me roll my eyes. Of all the girls, Sue's the one who gets over one man by getting under another. And she's given the advice freely to our tight group of friends. I can practically feel her elbow in my ribs.

"Yes, *Jacob*," I echo, mocking the way she said it, feeling irritable and juvenile, but it only makes Sue smile.

"Well I hope he's a good distraction for you," Sue says then winks and slides her bag off her lap, onto her shoulder.

"Work is always a good distraction." My tone destroys the bit of lightness. "I'm good at burying myself in it." The girls are quiet as my words sit stale in the air. It's part of the reason my marriage is tainted. I don't have to say it out loud and they don't have to tell me. Everyone already knows it.

She worked herself to death will be written on my tombstone. It's all I think while I stand at the counter and order another coffee. Regular this time, with a splash of cream and plenty of sugar.

"I read his book you gave me," Maddie says when I retake my seat a moment later, changing the subject back to Jacob Scott. "I looked him up online too," she adds as a smile spreads across her lips and her cheeks brighten with a blush. She scoots to the back of her seat and holds her cup in both hands, gladly taking the attention off of me. "He's cute," she says and smiles in a way I don't see often from her. My left brow raises as I watch her pink cheeks turn brighter. *Little Miss Innocent.*

"Is he now?" Sue comments and the two share a look as Maddie nods.

"Want me to put in a good word for you?" I question— it's meant for either of them really—and reach into my Kate Spade satchel for my laptop and notebook, setting them up on the table as Sue stands and puts on her jacket. There's no way Maddie would actually make a move. She's so sheltered and inexperienced. There's also no way I'd let someone like

Jacob near her.

"You can always stay and wait for him to get here?" I say jokingly. "Or maybe leave something behind and have to come back for it?"

She doesn't answer, merely shakes her head and slides off her seat to join Sue in leaving me to my fresh coffee and waiting laptop.

"I wouldn't want to impose," Maddie finally says and then walks over to give me a hug. Even in her heels, I still sit a little higher at the bar-height table as she embraces me.

I half expect her to say something in my ear, to tell me it'll be all right or that Evan's made a mistake. But she doesn't say a word until she lets me go. "I'm just a call away," she says with a chipper tone that wouldn't clue in anyone around us that I'd need to call her because my life is falling apart. Both of her hands grip my shoulders just a second too long.

My heart goes pitter-patter.

"Same here, darling," Sue adds, placing her own hand on Maddie's shoulder as a cue, and then the two walk off. The sound of Sue's heels starts to fade as she opens the door. But the chime sounds just the same as when we first walked in here.

"Later, loves." I force a smile on my face as they leave me here alone.

But my expression doesn't reflect anything I truly feel.

And nothing's changed.

Chapter 4

Evan

Berkeley Square in London feels the same as it has for years. The crisp air and old trees that tower over the park always feel timeless when I'm here. The black iron and white stone that speak to the history of this place never fail to impress. The dark, narrow alleys and the nightlife tucked away in the shadows of this city are what make my blood heat and my foot tap anxiously on the floorboard of the car.

It's always given me a rush to come here. There are a number of cities I'm fond of, cities that are playgrounds for the wealthy and where the best parties are had. Los Angeles, San Francisco, and New York City, of course. But London is one of the best. There's something to be said about being away from your normal life and getting to unwind in a city you don't have any obligations to stay in, yet welcomes you as if it's always been home.

The cabby clears his throat and his accent greets me as he tries to make small talk. I give him a curt nod and as many one-word answers as it takes to make it clear he doesn't need to fill the time with needless conversation. I'm not interested.

Rubbing sleep from my eyes, I lean back in the leather seat, feeling more and more exhausted as we pass the park, the dark green landscape fading from sight and rows of homes taking the place of the public areas.

I've felt comfortable here for years. It's a constant go-to for the PR company and I've been sent here to look after clients multiple times. But as the sky turns gray and the rain starts to beat against the tin roof, the welcoming feeling leaves me, and I'm left empty. Brought back to the present and brooding on how much the past has fucked me over.

The cab takes a left onto Hay Hill and I pass an old townhome where I used to crash. I've had so many close calls here. I was too much of a hothead, always looking for a thrill and pushing my luck further and further.

The cabby comes to a stop before I'm ready. The memories play on a loop in the back of my head of all the years I spent wasted. I can still feel the crunch of bone from the last fight I got into not three blocks from here.

"Here we are," the cabby states, turning in his seat, but

before he can say anything else, I jam some cash into his hand and grab my bags on my own.

"Have a good day, sir," I hear him call out as I shut the door, the patter of rain already soaking through my collar at the back of my neck.

I have to walk with my head down to keep the rain from hitting me in the face. The door opens easily and I drag my luggage in, tossing it to the right side where the coatrack and desk are meant to greet clients. This condo's been converted into an office space. It's blocks from the nightlife and blends in with the community. A perfect location for client drop-off.

The high ceilings and intricate crown molding make the already expensive building feel that much wealthier. It's all been done in shades of white and cream, without an actual color in sight. It makes the bright neon sticky note atop a stack of papers sitting on the edge of the welcome desk stand out even more.

Sterile, but rich.

"You were supposed to tell me when you landed." I hear James's voice before I see him, his heavy steps echoing in the expansive room.

"I did," I tell him flatly, not bothering to take out my phone and check. I'm positive I did, as I always do, and he ignored it. That seems to have been his preference for the last two weeks. The air about him has changed; ever since that night, things have been tense between us. As if we're in a silent war, each waiting for the other to show weakness.

I'm not interested in this shit. The only thing I give a damn about is my Kat, keeping her safe from the crossfire. So I'll play nice. I'll do what he says. But I'm not his bitch and I don't play games.

"I didn't get it," he says, stopping in front of me in the foyer. He has to tilt his head back slightly to look me in the eyes since he's a few inches shorter.

I shrug as if it doesn't matter, not bothering to confirm or deny whether a text was sent. "Well, I'm here now," I tell him as I slide off my jacket, soaked from the usual London rain, and hang it on the coatrack.

"You look like shit," he comments and an asymmetric grin tilts up my lips.

"Thanks." Running a hand over my damp hair and wiping it off on my jeans, I respond, "I'd say I feel better than I look, but that'd be a lie."

I've known James a long time, nearly a decade and I expect him to ask why, even though he already knows. I anticipate him starting the conversation, but instead he says nothing. Avoiding the obvious and walking down the hallway of the townhouse.

That's right, how could I forget? We're at war.

My feet move on their own, following him even though adrenaline courses faster in my blood. It makes me feel sick to not talk about it. To not clear the air.

"Whiskey?" he asks me as he pours himself a glass in the

converted dining room. It's more of a bar now with a long plank of cedar serving as a makeshift counter in the back of the room. The recessed lighting shines softly on the bottles of clear and amber liquids and creates an intimate feel in the room. The humidor full of Cuban cigars and pair of dark leather wingback chairs on either side of it must have been added after I was here last.

"Kane Buchan," he says, speaking the name and then hands me a manila folder. I'm sure it's filled with the same shit that was emailed to me. I've got Kane's profile memorized already. He was the lead singer in a rock band from the Bronx. They had one smash hit and then he split from the rest of them. He decided to go his own way thinking he was too good for the band. Most said it was his ego, but it turns out he was right. Three number one hits on the top record charts and now he's a client.

They all want the same. To flaunt their wealth, get drunk or high. Fuck whomever they want. Kane Buchan is no different.

"He said something about going to Annabel's tonight," James tells me and I nod my head. I've been there more than a time or two. It's exclusive and ridiculously overpriced, so of course an up-and-coming star wants to be seen there.

I already know exactly how the night's going to play out. I just have to keep it clean enough so there are no problems. Kane's had enough of them from the fallout with his previous drummer.

"Did you even hear what I said?" James asks in a raised voice laced with irritation.

"Annabel's," I answer as I look him in the eyes and hope he was still going on about the club.

"No, I said he's married now so make sure there are no pictures if he does something stupid."

"I know." That's a given.

"He's staying a few days, maybe less depending on what his agent wants. Just keep an eye on him, show him a good time—" He's pissing me off. Treating me like a new hire and nothing more.

"I know what to do," I say, cutting off James deliberately with my retort. "I've been here before."

I've had days to think of how to approach this, but I still hesitate to get everything off my chest.

He huffs a response, sounding something like disbelief and then grabs the tumbler of whiskey from the table. The ice clinks as he takes a sip and holds it in front of him.

"Buchan's agent doesn't need any more press other than what they've arranged."

"I want you to know," I start to say as I stare him in the eyes, forcing him to listen to what I'm telling him. "I think it was a setup." Maybe I'm paranoid, but I don't give a fuck. I have to tell someone. And I'm sure as shit not going to Samantha. "It was an accident, but it just doesn't seem right. Something's off."

He shrugs and says, "It was handled." He takes a sip of his whiskey before adding, "So I don't give a shit if it was."

"I do." My words come out hard and bitter, but James is already walking away from me. I know if I move an inch, if I even breathe, I'll beat the piss out of him for leaving this all on me. And risk losing everything.

Chapter 5

Kat

My bloodshot eyes hate me. They burn from the onslaught of cool air as I finally sit back down in my office. I'm always here. I never leave this room unless I have to.

When I do decide to perch on the sofa or go to bed, I always bring my laptop with me.

Workaholic is a word for it. I'm not sure even that does it justice. I gave up everything for this. For sitting in this damn office, making deal after deal.

It's why I came to New York.

It's why I spent years in the publishing industry, collecting contacts and building a brand that's recognizable. I do it on my own and it's always been rewarding. Up until recently, this was my dream.

While Evan stayed the same and carried on with a life that was a fun distraction, I buried myself in work. Growing farther and farther apart from my husband. Knowingly creating distance between us. I thought it was worth it and that they'd all understand.

Ignored friends ... at least I didn't have family to ignore. Other than Evan.

I rub my eyes again and try to soothe them, but the darkness is all I can see. It begs me to sleep.

I desperately need it. I can't even read an email right, partly from how tired my eyes are and partly from my inability to focus on anything at all. I've reread this pending message about a dozen times and I couldn't tell a soul what the content is to save my life. My meeting with Jacob is *next* week. I spent an entire hour on my own sitting mindlessly in the coffee shop before I bothered to check the time and date.

The errors are piling up and so is my anxiousness.

At least the coffee in the shop was comforting and the little biscuits were delicious. But the rain was coming down in sheets, and any sense of ease was gone by the time I dragged my ass back home to an empty townhouse with soaking wet jeans slick around my ankles.

My shoulders rise and fall as I take another glance at the screen. The contrast of the black and white is too harsh and I almost shut the laptop down and give in to sleep, but my phone goes off, scaring the shit out of me.

Evan.

It's my first thought and I hate how disappointed I am when I see it's not him. It's his father. My heart sinks and I pretend it doesn't hurt.

In my contact list, it still says "Evan's parents' house." It's tied to the number for the landline at the house where he grew up. He said he had the number memorized when he was only six years old.

Marie gave the number to me the night I first saw her, so she could call me about next Sunday's dinner, all those years ago. Every time I see the words *Evan's parents' house*, I'm reminded that only Henry remains.

It brings a number of memories I don't welcome. Just the same as the reminder of my own parents' sudden death in a car crash. Tragedy brought us together. It wasn't love. It was a need for love and that's something else entirely.

That's something Evan and I had in common, both of us losing our loved ones so quickly. He still has his father at least, but I've had no one for most of my life.

The phone rings and rings as I attempt to gather my composure. We'd only been seeing each other for a few months when I got the first call from this number. I was expecting it to be Marie, but it wasn't his mother making the call, it was Evan because his cell phone had died.

He told me he couldn't make it to our date and the first

thought I had was that he was breaking up with me, simply because of the tone of his voice. It wasn't until he apologized that I realized it was something else.

He couldn't hold it together on the phone. His voice shook and his sentences were short. I'll never forget that feeling in my chest, like I knew something horrible had happened and there was nothing I could do about it.

There was something in his voice that I recognized. It's how I sound when I'm trying to convince someone else I'm okay, but I'm not. I knew it well.

After my parents died, I got tired of having to convince people there was more to me than tragedy. People who didn't bother to get to know me, because I was just the sad girl at the end of the block. The *poor child* everyone talked about.

It was why I moved to New York. Living in the small town where my family died wasn't a healthy place for someone who just wanted to feel like there's something else in this world other than the past.

For Evan it wasn't a sudden car crash, it was the phrase "two weeks to live" that brought him to his weakest moment.

I insisted on seeing him and meeting him at his parents' place and even though I thought he'd object, he didn't. He'd never been so passive toward anything like he was that night.

Evan's only cried twice since I've known him.

That night after his mother had finally gone to bed and we went back to his childhood bedroom. And nineteen days later, when she was put in the ground.

My hand itches to hold his right now. Instead I hold a ringing cell phone in an empty home.

"Henry," I say, answering the phone as if nothing's wrong although I'm very aware my voice sounds nearly breathless. Clearing my throat, I repeat his name. My voice is peppy and full of life, even though it's nearly 10:00 p.m. and I feel nothing but dead inside.

I squint at the clock on the computer and wonder why he's calling so late. "Is everything all right?" I ask, rushing out the words, my heart beating slower and a deep fear of loss settling in.

"My favorite daughter-in-law," Henry says and his greeting makes a soft smile lift up my lips. I even feel the warmth from it.

"Your *only* daughter-in-law," I correct him, picking at a bit of fuzz on the sleeve of my shirt.

"Still my favorite," he replies and I give him the laugh that he's after, even if it is a little short and quiet.

"What are you calling for?" I ask him and rest my elbow on the desk, chin in my hand. I absently minimize the document on my screen and clear out all my tabs, checking my email yet again as Henry talks.

"I just wanted to check on you, make sure everything's going well."

Again, I get the sense that something's off. "That's sweet

of you," I tell him but before I can say everything's fine, he gets right to the real reason he called.

"You two all right?"

"Yeah," I say and instantly feel like shit. The single word is a vicious lie on my lips. I question what I should tell him: I don't know if my marriage to his son will last? That I'm falling apart and I have no idea how to make this better? That his son is a liar and I hate him for the pain he's putting me through?

"I spoke to Evan and he said he's not sure about the holidays coming up," Henry tells me and his tone reflects that he's baiting me. Henry's kind, polite, keeps to himself and doesn't want to be a bother, but he has a way of getting the truth out of people. Evan certainly inherited his charm from his father.

The screen of my laptop dims, ridding the room of any light so I hit the space bar and bring it back to life.

"It's a bit away, but," I say then pause and swallow, not knowing how to articulate the onslaught of thoughts. They all crowd themselves into a jam at the back of my throat, refusing to come out. I don't have family, so it's not as if I can use them as an excuse. "Work may be a little much." I finally say the words and breathe out slowly, giving him a lie I'm sure he knows is exactly that.

"He said you're going through something." There's no bullshit in his voice as he adds, "That you two aren't doing the best."

A pricking numbness dances across my hands as I ask weakly, "Did he?" Staring blankly ahead, the rhetorical question is like a knife in my back. It's a betrayal. That's how I feel hearing that Evan's told his father what we're going through. It makes the crack in my heart that much wider.

We aren't doing the best. I hear it over and over and each time the knife stabs deeper.

It's not fair that he invites so much attention. I don't need the judgment, because I don't want their opinions. I don't want them to know we're flawed. I just want us whole again. I wish no one knew so I could silently be the weak wife I am. The one willing to turn a blind eye for the unfaithful man she loves more than herself.

"I don't want to talk about it, Henry," I say bluntly as my eyes close at the confession. I can tell the computer has gone into sleep mode again and this time I don't hit the keys to bring it back to life. The darkness is too comforting.

"I just want you to know I'm here for you," Henry says clearly into the phone. "You're my daughter," he adds and it breaks my composure.

I push away from the desk, the chair legs catching on the rug and nearly tipping over. With a heavy inhale, I walk slowly to the door and then to my bedroom, the phone still pressed to my ear. I'm just going through the motions and trying to be numb to it all.

"Thank you," I finally say as I lean against the bedroom

door, closing it. I almost tell him he's like a father to me.

Almost, but when we do get a divorce, Henry won't be there for me. It doesn't matter what he says. It doesn't matter that I'll be alone, because that's how I've been most of my life anyway.

"I love you and I'm sorry you two are going through this." I let Henry's words echo in my head.

He's not the only one who's sorry.

Chapter 6

Evan

The music pounds away, the bass cranked up so high it vibrates my chest. The interior of the nightclub alternates between dark shadows and bright, colorful lights that flash in time with the beat. Vibrant reds and greens scatter across the slim bodies that come and go from sight with the sudden darkness in between the beats.

"Another!" Kane's friend Mikey yells on my left, a little too loud, a little too close to my ear for comfort. I give him a smile in return and pretend to take another swig of my beer. I'm used to guys like him.

Another time in my life, I'd actually be drinking. The feel that I get on the right side of a heavy buzz is comforting.

That light-headedness where you still have control, but not a damn thing matters. That's the place I craved to be for so long, but not anymore.

Not when so much is slipping through my fingers.

It's been a few hours since we got to Annabel's and so far the job's been easy. Kane and his friends are trashed and most importantly, the rock star is having the time of his life. His crew is saddled up to the bar with a few women pressing their bodies against the men who welcome it, letting their hands stray every so often. One in particular for Kane, which has me on edge and keeping an eye out for the telltale glow of a cell phone in the air, ready to capture a snapshot.

She's the woman closest to Kane, Christi is what she said her name was, and the loudest by far. The more she drinks, the louder she gets, and the closer to Kane. Not that Kane seems to notice any of that.

According to his file, the tall, loudmouthed blonde is his type and it wouldn't be the first time he's strayed from his wife. Fame and fortune tend to do it. I've seen it too many times to keep track.

Kat thinks this is the type of shit I do. The thought makes me sick to my stomach, a scowl marring my face. I can't change what my clients do; I learned that all too fast. You can't change people. You accept it and work with what you're given. A prick's a prick. He's never going to be anything but that. So I raise the beer to my lips and take a long swig, nearly draining the bottle.

With the change of music bringing the group a little closer as the lights fade, I watch them each carefully, but all I can think about is Kat. What she'd think of this mess.

She's never questioned me before, but last night she let out shit I had no idea about. Insecurities and accusations that made me feel like less of a man.

I can't blame her, can I? Not when I have secrets. Not when I can't look her in the eyes and tell her I haven't fucked up.

A strong grip on my arm rouses me from my thoughts.

"Can you get me something?" Kane asks, sidling up next to me. The smell of whiskey is heavy on his breath. It takes great effort not to put immediate distance between us.

Just like Mikey, he's a little too close as he slurs his request to the point where I can't tell what he's saying.

"What are you looking for?" I ask him to clarify and stare at the half-empty bottles of liquor lining the top shelf of the bar.

"Something a little stronger," he says as he tilts his head and tries to be subtle, but fails miserably, putting his hand to his nose and sniffing loudly. Cocaine.

I hesitate and waver on my answer. Luckily, I don't have to respond. Instead a loud, high-pitched voice on my right screams out, "We've got absinthe!" Apparently Christi was eavesdropping. *Surprise, surprise.* Her bright red talons are digging tight into Kane and I know she's going to stay within hearing range until we're out of here, just like she's been doing since she recognized him from across the room. She's leaning over a barstool, her breasts on full display and when I look back at Kane, the only thing he's looking at is her chest.

"Never had it," Kane says too low and the blonde screams, practically in my ear, "What?"

Giving them distance and getting out from between the two of them, I wait for him to agree. I know he will. She's got him wrapped around her little finger. I'll do it with a smile on my face and babysit this fucker. I used to think of this differently. This all used to be fun. But it wasn't like *this*, was it?

It doesn't take more than one feminine mewl and a *please* from her to convince Kane that absinthe is good enough and that we should all head to her place.

It's two blocks down and up a set of iron rails to get to the apartment. The sidewalk's still wet and this late at night, there's no one else on the streets. Just a bunch of drunk assholes stumbling on their way home. We fit in perfectly. I keep my eyes ahead, but occasionally look back and in all directions casually. I know the street and the apartment complex well. There aren't any cameras or storefronts for onlookers. Still, I watch and wait for any type of paparazzi.

I follow them as Kane and his friend cling to the group of women. There are three of them, two blond chicks and a dark brunette with curls, each barely covered in skimpy clubwear as they grip the railing to the apartment stairs and laugh as they stumble their way up in heels. It's difficult to tell with the other blonde if it's an act and she's playing up the drunkenness, or if she's really that plastered.

Kane's hands are all over Christi, moving from her hips to her ass as he walks behind her. Mikey's into the other blond chick and the brunette's checked out, only interested in smoking weed and getting trashed.

I tolerated the attention and flirting in the beginning of the night, but after a few minutes of ignoring the women, they lost interest and moved on. I'm certain this brunette is well aware there's nothing happening between us. The number one rule of my job is to not bring down the vibe. So I offer her a smile when she peeks at me, but then go back to scanning the surroundings and blocking the view from the street. One thought gnaws at me as the group travels along: I just want to get back to Kat and make her take it all back. Make her forget what happened and remind her why we're meant to be together. Remind her why she's mine.

I don't want this life anymore. Not when it makes Kat doubt me and what we have. Rightfully so.

I can't take this shit. I'll give it up for her. She'd take that, wouldn't she?

As the girls laugh nearly in unison to something that Mikey yelled out and the door opens, I take my phone out of my pocket, glancing up to make sure none of the girls have theirs out.

The number two rule of my job: no pictures.

That's my second concern. The first is getting Kane and peacing out of here. He's had a good time; he'll remember enough of it at least. I'm not interested in being here any longer than I have to be.

I'm distracted for only a moment. Half a second, but the moment I stop watching these girls, one of them breaks rule number two.

The second Christi's blond friend pulls out her iPhone, flicking her long hair behind her as if she's only taking a selfie, turning and posing with Kane in the background, I snatch it from her. She gasps and tries to grab it back like this is a game and I'm making a move on her. Her smile widens and she lets out a small laugh, again trying to snatch it from me.

Keeping the smile in place, I'm firm. It takes her a minute to realize no matter how much she pulls on my arm and makes that girlish cry, I have no intention of giving it back.

"No pictures," I tell her simply, my voice low and admonishing. I don't have time for this shit or her antics. She knows what she's doing and it's not cute or funny.

The smile drops from her face, her disappointment evident. I force myself to stare into her drunken hazel gaze until she looks down and then holds out her hand. The flirtation is completely gone. "I get it," she snaps.

I place the phone in her palm after I shut it off and she huffs like I'm an asshole, but she'll listen. They always do. It's obvious she's biting her tongue over wanting to tell me off and

I can't really blame her. She wouldn't be the first. I've been slapped more times than I know. Mostly by women. Years of doing this have led to plenty of fights and unfortunate events.

I've beaten the shit out of assholes.

Called doctors and paid them in cash to come to hotel rooms.

I've paid off cops, bouncers, bookies. At this point I've seen it all, done it all. And I'm tired of this shit.

This little blonde, though? She'll pout and listen, even if she tries to make a move on me and probably attempt even more pictures throughout the night.

The bright green of the absinthe bottle catches my eye as the blonde I just pissed off brings it to the coffee table. I watch as she sets it in the center and lines up three shot glasses before going back to the small kitchen only ten feet away to grab more.

Kane's in the middle of the sofa with both arms draped across the back as Christi and the brunette cuddle up next to him. The sounds of them laughing and Kane saying something in a low voice as they huddle closer to him are barely on my mind as I turn my focus back to my phone.

I text the driver and let him know I'm going to need the car in about thirty minutes then send him the address.

It takes fifteen minutes for the alcohol to hit their systems. Heavy pours and three shots each will have them all out on their asses. Normally I'd feel bad cutting their party short, but

I don't give a shit. All I can think about is Kat.

I need to get back to her.

With an asymmetric grin forced onto my face, I roll up my sleeves, letting the tats show. "Let me get it, doll," I tell the blonde as I make my way to the kitchen. "You sit back and relax," I add, taking the bottle from her hands. I'll pour the second round while they're throwing back the first. She gives me a flirtatious smirk. "I knew you weren't *all* asshole," she teases with a playful peek up at me and then sits on her knees next to the coffee table. Too close, too presumptuous.

"You had it right the first time," I murmur under my breath as I fill all six glasses and pass them out.

"Let's do a couple rounds and get this party started."

Chapter 7

Kat

"I'm stronger than this. I deserve so much more."
They're the words I breathe, then collapse on the floor.
My eyes close tight; tears trapped, lungs still.
I can't speak the truth; I can't fight the chill.
"I'm stronger than this." I whisper the words, my face hot.
But I know I'm a liar, and I know that I'm not.

Evan almost never texts me when he's working but he did tonight, and I can't take my eyes away from my phone because of that little fact. In all the years we've been together, I can count on one hand when he's messaged me while out on a job. I've never minded it; he's working. I've never needed a message that said he missed me, I always knew he did and that he'd be home soon. I had work to occupy me while he was away. Come morning, there was always a message to greet me, but while he was out, he was simply unavailable.

My body's still and my focus is nonexistent when it comes to work now, though. There's not a damn thing keeping me company but the memories of us and the constant worry of what'll happen when—and if—he comes home.

Staring down at my cell, I swallow thickly. *He messaged me. He reached out to me.* I can't explain why it makes my bruised heart hurt even more. Maybe I wish he'd just be cruel and not try or not care. It hurts so much more to think that he's trying. Hope is an odd little thing. I want to cling to it, but if I do, the inevitable fall will be that much more deadly.

He always messaged in the morning, though, after the late night of whatever the hell he'd been up to. I've always thought it was cute how he'd text me to tell me good morning, even if he was only just then getting into bed.

But it's 2:00 a.m. in London, his prime time, and my phone's lit up on the desk with a message from him.

I was finally getting some work done, the keys clacking and the to-do list shrinking somewhat although for every item crossed off, I feel as if I've added two. Focusing and managing to write up some feedback along with creating a marketing tactic for a client has been a highlight of my night ... Until that message came through.

Half of me doesn't want to answer him. Cue the grinding halt to any progress I'd made. I don't want to read whatever he's sent and go back into the black hole of self-pity. But I can't resist. He is a drug and I am an addict. We could go days without speaking before, but in this moment, every second that I stare at my phone knowing there's an unread message from him feels like an eternity in hell.

My hand inches toward it, the need to see what he has to say overriding the anger and the sadness. The need to be wanted by him and to feel loved winning out over my dignity.

So I click on the damn thing and my heart does a little pitter-patter of acknowledgment. When I swallow, it's as if I'm shoving my heart back down where it belongs.

I hate it when you're mad at me.

I stare at his message, feeling the vise in my chest tighten. My fingers hesitate over the keys as I read it again and again. Before I can respond, another message comes through.

Forgive me.

That's the crux of the situation. The dams break loose.

Forgive you for what exactly? I message him back without even thinking. Whatever he's hiding is bad, I know it is. I can feel it deep down in my core. Just like I knew that night when his mother was diagnosed. Whatever he's done is enough to ruin us.

But we were already ruined, weren't we? It's been a slow burn of destruction. My intuition is hardly ever wrong. We've grown apart. We're different people now. *We don't belong together.* We never did, not really. Admitting that is what hurts the most.

With my body trembling, I force myself to get up and move, even if it's just to walk through the house. I'm only wearing a baggy shirt and a pair of socks. I wore the shirt to bed last night and I should really shower and get dressed. It's a rule I've had since I started working from home.

Every day, I dress as if I'm going into the office. Right now I just don't have the energy.

Evan sends two texts, one right after the other as I walk to the kitchen.

We can work through this.

I love you.

I only glance at them before putting the phone down on the counter and heading straight to the fridge for some wine. Taking in a staggered breath, I focus on ignoring the pain. *Think logically*, I command myself. *Don't fall back into his arms without having a grasp on the problem. Because otherwise it will happen again. That's what happens when you accept a behavior without acknowledgment and a plan to change.*

There's only half a glass left in the dark red bottle, but it'll have to do.

I glance at the clock as I sip it. It's after 9:00 p.m. I've barely slept, barely worked and hours passed before I realized I hadn't brushed my teeth today. At least I'm drinking from a clean glass.

It only takes one sip before I tell him what's on my mind. Communication is key. All the years of therapy taught me that. There is no relationship worth keeping if you don't trust what someone says.

I don't understand why you won't tell me what you did.

Won't tell you what? he texts back and it pisses me off.

"Does he think I'm stupid?" I mutter beneath my breath as my blood boils. The anger is only an ounce stronger than the pain. In the back of my mind I note that only crazy people talk to themselves, but even if that's the case, I accept it. This man makes me crazy. I can admit that much.

Don't treat me like this, I answer him, feeling weak. I'm practically begging him in my head but when I reread the text it sounds strong. *I deserve better.*

I down the remaining wine after sending the last line, the cool red soothing a tiny bit of an ache. I don't know exactly what it is I deserve but I have a rough idea. Him telling me the truth. Him confiding in me. Or a better husband altogether.

As I grab the last bottle of red wine on the rack and bring it back to the kitchen, I realize this is how women feel when they stay in these marriages.

They'd rather be told a sweet little lie and believe it than face the truth. Those are my choices: demand the truth and accept the lie he gives me or ... I don't know.

Right now, it's exactly what I want. Just lie to me. Tell me there's nothing that happened. That it's blown out of proportion. *That it was just a kiss.* Yes, that one. That last one. I could forgive it, but better yet, I could believe it. I could allow myself to believe it, even if deep down inside I know it was more.

Lie to me and love me. He knows I'll still love him. It would make everything better.

The barstool legs scratch on the floor as I sit down to uncork the new bottle.

I just want him to come home. Tell me everything is fine and make up something that's easy to forgive. It was only a kiss.

With a bottle of wine and a full glass in front of me, I go back to the beginning. Back to when I was stronger and I actually had self-respect.

Back to when I knew better.

The memory and the wine are the only things to keep me company for the rest of the night, because Evan doesn't text me back with the truth or a lie. He gives me silence.

Six years ago

The wind blows in my face, alleviating some of the stifling summer heat as I pull into the gas station parking lot in Brooklyn. It's late and the hustle and bustle of New York has waned, but the nightlife on this side of the city is only getting started.

Some would say it's the bad part of town, but others say it's the fun part. I guess it depends on what circles you run in. New to New York and struggling to find where I belong,

I suppose I'm keeping an open mind. The bright lights and sophistication are what I came here for, but making it here isn't so easily achieved.

I'm slow to step on the brakes and pull into the last spot that lines the front of the small convenience store. I've only been here a few times, either needing to stop for gas or a quick bite to eat on my way to or from work on the west side of the city. It's a clerical job for a newspaper, but beggars can't be choosers and the bills need to be paid while I learn the ropes, snag clients and rub elbows, so to speak.

Several cars are parked in front of the store and a few men head inside as I pull up. They vary from obviously expensive to looking like they're falling apart. The vehicles, that is.

I notice the men, and they notice me. Averting my eyes to avoid making small talk, I turn down my radio and put my car in park.

I mind my business and everyone around me seems to do the same. In the city that never sleeps, there's always something happening. And I'm not interested in a damn one of those somethings. Distractions get a bad rap for a reason.

Grabbing my purse and keys in the same hand, I make haste, opening the car door to step out in a rush, but my eyes glance back to the cars and straight into a man's gaze.

Not just any man, a man exuding power and confidence, along with defiance. Although he's wearing a simple shirt and faded dark jeans, the way he wears them makes me think they were made to be fitted to his muscular body. He's hot as hell, and given the way he looks at me, he could be a temptation the devil made just for me.

My driver's side door shuts with a loud bang as I stand there caught in the heat in his gaze. He leans against the hood of a car, I'm assuming is his, a shiny black Mercedes that reflects the light from the store in its slick exterior. The windows are rolled up and tinted so dark it's hard to see the inside. As my eyes move back to the man, my movements are slowed and I grip my keys tighter.

He doesn't stop looking, taking me in and letting his eyes follow along the curves of my body. Arrogance and sinful thrill dance in his cocky grin. He obviously wants me to know that he's watching me. Something about that small fact forces a blush to rise to my cheeks.

My breathing picks up and I subconsciously pull the hem of my dress down just slightly, smoothing out the cherry red pleats and wishing I hadn't been wearing it all day. I take one step and the click of my heels keeps time with my racing pulse as I walk forward, knowing I have to pass him on my way in.

I can't help that my eyes flicker over to his as I grip my purse strap and settle it in place. His shirt is pulled taut and over his muscular frame and his tanned skin is decorated with ink. Tattoos travel down his chest and arms, peeking out below his collarbone from the crisp white cotton shirt and leaving a trail of intricate designs all the way down to his wrists. I'm too far away to see what they say or what they are. I know if he were in a suit, the tattoos would be hidden, but something tells me he's proud to have them on full display.

"What are you up to?" he asks me and catches me off guard.

"I don't think that's any of your business," I answer him easily, although I don't know how, swaying a little from side to side in a flirtatious way I didn't intend. My body can't help but be attracted to his. Some part of me is eager to know how his tattooed skin would feel against my fingertips.

There's a scar over his left eyebrow and it's subtle, but even from this distance I notice it. As his deep rough chuckle fills the night air and drowns out the other sounds of the city, I find myself wondering how he got it.

"A man can wonder, though," he says, causing a hot blush to creep slowly into my cheeks. I bite down on my lower lip, but that doesn't stop the shy smile from showing. I have to stop and give him the attention he's looking for as he leans forward, holding me captive to whatever's on his mind.

"You're pretty, you know that?" he says and I roll my eyes. Even if I know this flirtation isn't just for me, that he's simply playing with me, I still enjoy it. I crave it even. I'm sure he's already used these lines tonight.

"Sure, and you're not too bad looking either." I enjoy the flirting, the attention. At least coming from him. He makes me feel things I haven't before.

He splays a hand over his heart and cocks his head as he says,

"Well thank you, beautiful, I aim for 'not bad.'" This time I'm the one laughing, a short, soft snicker as I kick the bottom of my heels against the ground and stare at them for a moment, readying myself to say goodbye and end his bout of teasing. I don't trust myself not to say anything and instead I just wave and carry on, expecting him to do the same.

"You didn't answer me," he calls out after I take a few steps. "What are you doing out here so late?" he asks. It's forward of him and I usually despise that, but instead I savor the challenge in his voice. Something about it tells me he thinks I'm already his. And that ownership makes my blood that much hotter.

I know I shouldn't give him any information at all, but I find myself telling him the truth before I can stop myself. "I'm hungry and overworked. So I stopped to grab a bite to eat."

"You're getting your dinner from here?" he asks, gesturing to the store and I nod. "A woman like you should be taken out, not eating dinner from the gas station."

A woman like you *plays over and over in my head. He doesn't know what type of woman I am. "You don't even know my name," I say, the half smile and challenge firm on my expression.*

He nods and grins, flashing me a cocky smile as he replies, "Don't make me guess."

I chew on my lip for a moment, rocking from side to side. He's bad news and I'm flirting with fire ... but I love the thrill. I can't deny it. "It's Kat," I tell him and a smile is slow to form on his face. One of complete satisfaction, as if hearing my name is the best thing that's happened to him all night.

"I'm Evan," he says and I taste his name on the tip of my tongue, nearly whispering it. "Let me take you to dinner, Kat," he suggests with an easiness I don't like. I wonder how many times that's worked for him before.

"I'm not your type," I respond, intentionally looking past him at the bars that wrap around the glass door to the convenience store. I just need a late-night snack to hold me over till morning. That's all this little errand was supposed to turn into.

"I don't think you should tell me what is and isn't my type." Although it comes out playful, there's a hint of admonishment, and my naïve little heart doesn't like that. "You might be surprised," he adds.

I clear my throat and try to breathe evenly, wanting this flirting session to end so I can get back to work. I have to admit the attention is very much appreciated, though. And the desire in his eyes looks genuine.

"Sorry, Charlie, didn't mean to upset you," I tell him with a playful pout as I walk past him.

"It's Evan," he says, repeating his name and that makes a wicked grin play at my lips, "and you're wrong." The last part is spoken with a seriousness I wasn't expecting. His tone is hard and when I turn around to face him fully, finally taking a step onto the curb, he's no longer leaning on the hood of the Mercedes. He takes a few strides across the asphalt parking lot and stops in front of me as I ask, "Wrong about what?"

Up close he's taller than I first thought, more intimidating too and his shoulders seem broader, stronger. Even his subtle moves as he brushes his jaw with his rough fingers and licks his lower lip again, are dominating. He glances to the left and right before opening his mouth again and letting that deep, rough voice practically ignite the air between us.

"You're wrong that you aren't my type and that I'm not your type."

The compliment makes my body feel hotter than it already is in the hot summer night. Someone behind me exits the store, the telltale jingle of the bells and the whoosh of air-conditioning reminding me that I'm supposed to be in and out of this store. Reminding me that Evan isn't a part of my to-do list tonight.

"I never said you weren't my type," I say and my voice comes out sultry, laced with the desire I feel coursing in my blood. I try to hold his gaze, but the fire and intensity swirling in his dark eyes make me back down.

I can try to be tough all I want, but he's a bad boy through and through and I should know better.

"Good to know," he says with a cocky undertone that makes my eyes whip up to his. I half expect him to blow me off now that his ego's been fed. He licks his lower lip and my eyes are drawn to the motion, imagining how it'd feel to have his lips on every inch of my skin. "Come out with me tonight," he says. As if I don't have anything better to do. As if he can just command me to do what he wants.

"Sorry ... Evan. I can't tonight," I tell him and turn back around, hiking my purse up higher on my shoulder, ready to go about my business.

"Tomorrow night then," he says, raising his voice so I can hear him as I wrap my hand around the handle and pull the door open. Again the chill of the store greets me, but this time it's unwanted.

I'm all too aware of what this man could do to me. He's the type to pin you down as he takes you how he wants you and doesn't stop until you're screaming. And I can't lie, just that thought alone makes me desperate to say yes.

He takes another step closer as I stand with the door wide open and hesitate to answer. Shoving his hands into his pockets, he manages a shrug as if it's a casual question.

"Just one date," he adds as he looks at me with a raised brow and his version of puppy dog eyes. It's enough to force a smile on my face.

"And what am I supposed to do? Meet you here at ten?" I ask him.

"How about at Jean-Georges in Central Park?" he asks and I'm taken aback. It's an expensive place and my eyes glance back to his car, to his ripped body and tattooed skin. There's something about the air that follows him that screams he's no good. The danger in the way he looks at me is so tempting, though.

"I just want to feed you," he adds as the time ticks by slowly and a short, older man with salt-and-pepper hair walks out of the exit, stealing our attention and making my hand slip slightly on the handle.

I chew on the inside of my cheek. The answer is an easy one. No. Simple as that. He's a bad boy who only wants one thing, but I can't deny that I want it too.

I said yes.

To the date, and then again a year later to marrying him.

That initial yes, pushed through my lips by an undeniable attraction, was my first mistake on a list of too fucking many.

All because I can't tell him no.

Chapter 8

Evan

I try to shut the front door softly, as quietly as I can so I don't wake up Kat if she's passed out.

I know she told me not to come back. She says a lot of things and then apologizes and changes her mind. Silence isn't better, though. It still hurts, just in a different way. Our loft is small and the walls are thin so you can hear everything in here. I stop in the foyer, setting down my duffle bag and luggage then toss the bunched-up chenille blanket that's in a puddle on the floor onto the sofa in the living room.

The room is mostly gray, just like the city. There's a paned glass mirror above the long sofa and black and white accents everywhere. I hated that mirror from the moment we got it, but Kat loved it, so I never said a word. It belongs in some farmhouse up north, not in the heart of New York, the devil's playground. But it made her smile. I'll be damned if that isn't reason enough to keep that cheap-ass mirror.

My eyes scan the room in the faint light from the city that's shining through the gap in the curtains.

Five years of marriage, six of creating this place together.

Each piece of furniture is a memory. The wine rack that we purchased was the first thing we bought together. The gray sofa with removable pillows was a fight I lost. I didn't want the cushions to be removable, because they always end up sagging, but Kat insisted the brand was quality.

The plush cushions still look like they did in the store, and I wonder if she was right or if it's just because we don't even sit on the damn thing. Maybe both but I lean toward the latter.

I'm never here and she's always working. What's the point of it?

The bitter thought makes me kick the duffle bag out of my way and head past the living room and dining room, straight to the stairs so I can get to bed and lie down with Kat. It's been almost a week since I've slept in the same room as her and I refuse to let that go on for another night. I pause to look at the photos on the wall, the light streaming in leaving a sunbeam down the glass.

Almost all are in black and white, the way Kat likes her

décor. All but one, the largest in the very center. It's also the only one that's not staged.

She's leaning toward me, and her lips look so red as she's mid-laugh, holding a crystal champagne flute and wrapping her fingers around my forearm. Her eyes are on whoever was giving a speech. I don't remember who it was or what they said, but I can still hear her laugh. It's the most beautiful sound.

She was so happy on our wedding day. I thought she'd be stressed and worried, but it was like a weight was lifted and the sweetest version of her was given to me that day. There's nothing but love in the photo. No work, no bullshit, just the two of us telling the world we loved each other enough to stay together forever.

My eyes are on her in that picture, with a smile on my face and pride in my reflection.

I tear my gaze away and keep walking, feeling the weight of everything press down on my shoulders. I'm exhausted and like the childish fool I am, I wish I could just go to sleep and this would all be a dream. A huff of sarcasm accompanies my gentle footsteps up the stairs.

I want to go back to when we first got married. Before we both got caught up in work and started to live separate lives. Before I fucked up.

If only we could start over and go back to that day.

As I pass the open office door, I hear the clacking of the computer keyboard. So many nights I've come home to this, so many mornings I've woken up to it. She's always in her office, which is a shame. There's hardly any light, or anything at all in the room. File cabinets, papers, a shredder and a desk. There's not a hint of the woman Kat is in this room.

I guess it's the same as the living room, but at least a classic elegance is present there. It's nothing but cold in here. If a to-do list could be made into décor, that's what this cramped room resembles.

"Hey, babe," I say softly and Kat ignores me. I clear my throat and speak louder. "I'm home," I tell her and again, I get nothing from Kat, just the steady clicks. There's an empty wineglass and two bottles on the floor by her feet.

Maybe she's a little drunk, maybe she has her earplugs in too, but still, she'd hear me. Was it a long shot that she'd kindly accept me coming home? *Yes.* It's not too much to ask for an acknowledgment, though. Even if she tells me to fuck off. I'd take it.

My teeth grind together as I grip the handle of the door harder. She deserves better. I know she does. This is exactly what I deserve, but I don't want it. I won't go down without fighting for what I want.

The standing floor lamp in the corner of her office is on, but it's not enough to brighten the room. Even the glow of the computer screen is visible.

"Do you want to talk?" I ask her and her only response is that her fingers stop moving across the keys.

She doesn't turn to face me or give any sign that I've spoken to her. She heard it, though, and her gaze drops to the keyboard for a second too long not to give that away.

"I don't want to fight, Kat," I tell her and force every bit of emotion I'm feeling into my words. "I don't want this between us."

She turns slowly in her seat, a baggy T-shirt covering her slim body and ending at her upper thighs. Her exposed skin is pale and the dark room makes her look that much paler. Her viridian eyes give her away the most, though. Nothing but sadness stares back at me.

My body is pulled to her, and I can't help it. I can't stand that look in her eyes. Before I can tell her I love her and I'm sorry, before I can come up with some lame excuse, she cuts me off.

"I wanted to last night," she says and then crosses her arms. She looks uncomfortable and unnatural. Like she's doing what she thinks she should be doing, not what she wants. "When you texted me and then I texted you back. I was ready to talk then."

"I'm here now," I offer and walk closer to her, the floorboards creaking gently. There's a set of chairs in the corner of the room from our first apartment and I almost drag one over, but I'm too afraid to break eye contact with her. It's progress. I'll be damned if I stop progress for a place to sit.

At least she's looking at me, talking to me, receptive to what I have to say.

"Ask me whatever you want." My voice is calm but deep down I'm screaming. Because I know I'll answer her. I'll tell her everything just to take that pain away, even if it's only temporary, even if it fucks her too.

Her doe eyes widen slightly and she cowers back, swallowing before answering me. "Aren't you tired?" she says softly and her eyes flicker to the door and then to the floor.

She doesn't want to know the truth.

"Yeah, I'm exhausted. But I'm not going to bed until you do." I lick my lips and clear my throat, hoping she'll give in to me. For nearly the past year when I'm home, I've tried to stay up with her or brush off the fact that I'd pass out while she was still working and vice versa. Not tonight, not from this point forward. The advice my father gave me on our wedding night was to go to bed together. I should have listened. I'll make it better, I can at least fix that.

"I can stay up for you," I say, offering her the suggestion. It's not what she wants, but it's something.

"Well, this has to get done, and it's going to take hours."

"I can wait," I tell her but the second the words slip out she turns back to the computer and says, "Don't."

With her back to me and her fingers already flying across the keys again, I've never felt more alone and crestfallen.

"I'll go unpack and relax on the bed then," I say as I grip the doorframe to stay upright and keep myself from ripping her out of that chair and bringing her to bed.

"Here?" Shock coats the single word.

It takes me a moment to realize why the hell she's asking me that and when I do, it's like a bullet to the chest.

A mix of emotions swell in my gut and heat my blood. Anger is there, but the dejectedness is what cuts me the most.

"Is that all right?" I ask sarcastically.

She nods, conceding to let me stay in my own damn house, but the look in her eyes doesn't fade. She really wants me out. She wants me to just leave? Did she think I wouldn't fight for her? That I'd let this destroy us? It may ruin me, but I'd rather chew on broken glass than let it ruin *us*.

"I said I don't want a divorce." My words come out hard. I'm sick of this. "I want you," I tell her with conviction and walk closer to her, not leaving any space between us.

"I don't know what I want," Kat responds in a murmur, gripping the armrests of the desk chair as her lips form a painful frown and her eyes gloss over. Like she's on the verge of breaking. The last thread that was holding her together has snapped, leaving her falling. I'm not there to catch her, because I'm the one that pushed her over the edge. I hate myself for it.

It's my fault, and this is all on me, but I'll make it right.

"You don't have to, Kat," I say, softening my voice and moving just a little closer. I need a chance. She's vulnerable; I can feel it coming off of her in waves. *Give in to me, baby.*

I cup her cheek in my hand to lean down and kiss her, but

she pushes back, quickly standing and making the chair slam against the desk.

My pride, my ego, whatever it is that makes me a man, is destroyed in this moment. My limbs freeze and the tension makes me feel like I'm breaking. Literally cracking in my very center.

I lick my lips, finally letting out a breath as Kat whispers, "I'm sorry, I'm just ..." She doesn't finish, and I have to look up at her before I can stand upright again.

"You just what?"

"I don't know, Evan," she answers with desperation in her voice.

"Don't think," I tell her, grasping for anything to keep her from running. "Just let me make it better," I offer and she stands there, in nothing but that T-shirt, and looks at me as if I'm both her savior and her enemy.

I walk slowly, each step making the floor groan in quiet protest. I don't quicken my pace until I'm close enough to her to feel her heat. And she lets me, standing still and giving me the chance I need.

My lips crash against hers, my body molding to her small frame and forcing her back. For each step she takes, I take one with her.

"Stop," she tells me and pushes me away. My breathing is ragged as my hands clench to keep from holding on to her as she leaves me. I can still taste her, my body ringing with desire to make it up to her.

To ease her pain and remind her how good I make her feel. It's what she needs. It's been weeks and I can't deny I need her even more. I need to bury myself inside her warmth.

My hands grasp her hips and I push her back against the wall. Her arms wrap around my neck as she comes in for the kiss this time. Taking the passion from me, letting me give her what she needs. Comfort and an escape from reality. A welcome distraction to the fact that our marriage is at risk.

Right now there's nothing but what we feel for each other. Nothing else. No logic or reason. Just the devotion and intense desire.

I'm grateful it still exists. I only wish this moment would last forever. Where we're both weak for each other, desperate and drunk with lust.

"You're mine, Kat," I whisper against the shell of her ear. My breath is hot and it's making the air between us that much hotter.

Her back arches against the wall and she pushes her soft curves into mine. A quiet moan spills from her sweet lips. I stare at her face, the expression of utter rapture with her eyes closed and her lips parted just slightly.

I rock my palm over her again and again, putting pressure on her swollen nub and feeling her cunt get hotter and wetter.

"This is mine," I whisper louder, not holding back the possession in my voice.

A strangled moan fills the air. At first I don't know if it's from me or her, but the sweet cadence of her voice prolongs the sound of pleasure as her body writhes against mine. She's so close.

I tear the thin lace fabric of her panties off in one tug after ripping it with my thumb and watch her face as her eyes pop open. The gorgeous greens stare back at me with a mix of emotions, the overwhelming two being desire and vulnerability.

I don't give her the chance to second-guess this. This is how we're meant to be. Together, raw and bared.

I only release my grip on her to unzip my pants. The sound mixes with Kat's heavy breathing.

"Evan," she says, whispering my name as if it's a question.

She wants me, although she knows we shouldn't do this. Fuck, I know she's going to question this. Maybe even regret it. But she just needs to feel me again; she needs this as much as I do.

I press the head of my dick against her opening and slide myself through her slick folds, teasing her and watching as her eyes close tight. She squirms when I just barely touch her clit.

So close.

"Evan," she whispers again and this time it's a plea. One I can satisfy.

In one swift stroke I slam into her all the way to the hilt, making her scream out.

Her blunt nails dig into my shoulders as her body is forced against the wall and her head falls back.

I kiss her throat ravenously, desperate to taste her, but not willing to mute the sounds of pleasure she's making.

My thrusts are primal, ruthless. I take from her over and over. Each time her back hits the wall, her whimpers get louder and louder.

Her grip tightens as my balls draw up. My spine tingles with the need to release, but I need her to find hers with me. I'm desperate to feel her walls tighten around my cock. Desperate to feel her pulsing and lost in pleasure.

The moment I think I can't take any more, she gives me what I need. Screaming out my name as her orgasm rips through her body.

"Fuck," I groan into the crook of her neck. My dick pulses and I come hard, buried deep inside of her. My heart hammers hard and fast and refuses to stop as she clings to me for dear life. A cold sweat lines my skin. Her eyes are closed and her teeth are digging into her bottom lip when I finally look at her.

"I love you, Kat," I whisper as I pull away from her, finally breathing and starting to come down from the highest high.

"I love ..." Kat starts to reply, but she doesn't finish. She doesn't look me in the eyes.

She's so ashamed to love me, she can't even say it back.

Chapter 9

Kat

I don't know what I'm more ashamed about as I carelessly toss the throw blanket over one arm of the sofa and force myself get up, still feeling the ache between my thighs.

The fact that I fucked my husband.

Or the fact that I then refused to go to bed with him.

Not that I told him so much. I hid behind work and then snuck out here to the living room. I didn't sleep on the sofa for more than a few hours. Maybe that's all I'm entitled to for being so weak and falling right into his arms the moment he pulled me in.

It's like our union is a spiraling dark hole and I'm falling deeper and deeper, to the point where what I want and what

I'm feeling don't make sense and nothing adds up. Not that I could hold on to anything anyway; I've lost all control.

I couldn't possibly feel more pathetic at this point.

Because I love him and hate myself for it.

I glance at my phone on the dining room table as I make my way to the kitchen, the charging cord is in a tangled heap on the floor.

I already know what Sue would say. She'd feel sorry for me for going back to the man who cheated on me. Her lips would purse in that way where it's obvious she's holding back some snarky remark.

Pity and sorrow for the pathetic girl, clinging to an unfaithful man. Even the bitter thought echoes what I already know she'd say.

The thing about love though is that it's not a light switch. You can't just turn it off. No matter how much you may want to, you can't erase the memories and move on. Sue knows that much, she just chooses to forget that it's not so easy.

My head throbs and I'm not sure if it's from the lack of sleep or the absence of caffeine. Even the faint sounds of city life from stories down are enough to make my temples pulse. I've felt more put together with a hangover than I do now. This is not the unfortunate side effect of too much cabernet last night. I wish it was only that.

I groan as I rest against the wall of the living room and try to calm the headache. I close my eyes and feel the weight of all the stress from the last two weeks.

I need aspirin or coffee. Or both. My heart sputters as I slowly walk up the stairs, knowing Evan's lying in bed alone and that it was my choice.

As I pass the office, I remember last night and my thighs clench; I can still feel him inside of me. His warm lips on my neck, his rough hands on my body... it's more than a memory, the act still lingers on my skin. He took from me. Relentlessly, possessively. Each step brings my body temperature higher and higher, yet my heart hurts more and more.

Why won't the pain just go away? Why can't my head just shut the fuck up so I can pretend I'm okay for a single moment? Jules told me once I overthink everything. She was referring to some edits I gave her but still, the woman had a point.

The bedroom door is open and as I walk through the door, I can't take my eyes off the perfectly made bed. The cream and white comforter printed with black dahlias is pulled tight, looking pristine. A crease forms in the center of my forehead as I walk to the bathroom, listening to my heart beat with each step, but finding the bathroom empty. *Evan wasn't downstairs*, I think as I open the medicine cabinet and silently grab a bottle of aspirin. He wasn't downstairs, and he's not up here.

I swallow the pills without water, staring into the mirror as my heart clenches, the dark bags under my eyes looking significantly worse than yesterday morning. Did he even stay last night? Did he find me asleep on the sofa and decide to leave? *It's what I wanted, wasn't it?*

The cabinet door slams shut; I give the push more force than I meant to, but I ignore it, striding quickly down to the kitchen, the baggy T-shirt flowing around my thighs as one sleeve slips down my shoulder.

I just need coffee. Coffee will wake me, rid me of this headache and give me the energy I need to deal with this mess.

It is such a chaotic mess; I'm not sure how it possibly got worse than it was. A mix of emotions and desires that thrashes me side to side like an unforgiving earthquake. The only thing certain is that I can't stand on my own two feet. At least not without a cup of coffee.

A sarcastic huff of a humorless laugh leaves me as I round the bottom of the stairs and head to the kitchen, a pitiful smile adorning my lips. Ask and you shall receive; I'm a spiteful self-fulfilling prophecy.

All the plans I had are threatening to blow away like the stubborn seeds of a dandelion. Marriage, traveling, success and recognition. Then what? A small bump at my stomach cradled by his hand on top of mine.

Using the wineglass from last night I left next to the sink, I fill it with water and pour it into the back of the coffee maker, remembering the days when having a child was on my mind. Back when my career was only a long shot of a dream, when my time was monopolized by Evan and we owned the world together. We could be and do anything we wanted.

I slip a fresh coffee pod into the machine and turn it on as I remember how he'd hold my belly and plant a kiss there, just below my belly button, telling me what a wonderful mother I would be one day to his son.

With my throat tight I admit one thing: *we were fools.* I knew this would never last. I knew it back then. Just like I know it now.

I bite the inside of my cheek and take in a heavy breath, slipping the ceramic mug with *Rise and Shine* scrolled on the side under the spigot to the coffee machine.

My bare feet pad on the tiled kitchen floor as I open the fridge and search for the creamer, ignoring the old dreams and memories being dredged up. I stare longer than I should at the empty spot on the shelf. *I can't even remember to get creamer.* My teeth grind back and forth and the throbbing comes back with a vengeance to my temples.

I slam the fridge door shut as the coffee maker sputters to life. It's quite something when you've fallen so hard that a mundane task like going to the grocery store is enough to push you over the edge. Maybe I've truly gone crazy.

The creak of the front door opening is the last thing I need right now. The door closes softly, as if Evan didn't want to wake me. I wipe under my eyes and push my hair out of my face as I lean against the wall with my arms crossed, waiting for him to make his way in here.

I can't explain why I feel guilty. It's all I feel, like everything I've done is wrong and I'm the one to blame. Is this normal? I feel like this is what I deserve. Like somehow I've orchestrated all of this just so I could feel lonely and miserable. Maybe I had it too good and I decided I needed to go right back to the mental space where I used to feel like I was drowning.

"Morning." I hear Evan's voice and the sound of a plastic bag crinkling before I see him.

My lips part to tell him good morning, but then I catch sight of him.

He looks tired, his scruff a little too grown out, his dark hair a little too long and a bit of darkness under his eyes. For the first time I've laid eyes on him, he looks older, more mature but still as handsome as ever.

It all brings me to an abrupt halt. His jaw tenses as he rests the bag on the counter and then looks over his shoulder at me. "Did you sleep well?" he asks, barely looking at me before turning his attention to the corner cabinet and grabbing a mug for himself.

"No," I say, forcing out the word. "Evan ..." I try to keep talking but my heart slams at the same time that Evan shuts the cabinet and turns around to face me. He leaves the stark white mug on the granite countertop where it clinks in protest, and I stare at it, rather than at him.

I have to spend time away from him. That's what I need. To get used to being alone again and stopping this back and forth.

"I need you to leave," I tell Evan evenly and then peek up at him. It hurts to say the words after last night. I should have said them before, but I was so tired and felt so alone. It was selfish to need him then. I used him in a way, but I won't do it again. I won't keep pretending.

He shakes his head, not once or twice but continuously as if he's in disbelief. Like I didn't actually tell him that. He had to know it was going to come to this.

"Last night—"

"Was a mistake," I say, cutting him off forcefully and my voice cracks. My chest feels tight and it's harder to breathe, but I stand my ground.

"We're different people, Evan." I try to say more but my words are stuck in my throat, threatening to choke me.

"We've always been different, Kat. Always," Evan says and his words come out hard. I can already hear him convincing me. I can already see myself falling right back into his arms because that's where I feel so safe and so loved. But he can't hold me forever.

"I can't do this, Evan," I tell him honestly, feeling my heart break as I voice the words. It's a slow break, one meant to be torturous.

"Do what?" he asks me cautiously and it pisses me off. The plastic bag rustles as he reaches behind him, brushing against it and bracing himself against the counter.

"This. I can't." I look him in the eyes even as mine water.

I let the tears fall as my blood turns to ice, yet my skin heats.

Evan takes a step toward me, my name falling from his lips as his arms open and spread wide.

"If you won't tell me the truth about what happened, you need to get out."

With his eyes still widening, he shakes his head, an apology from his subconscious before he has the chance to say the words himself.

"Get out!" I yell at him, feeling the weakness threatening to consume me. Threatening to bring me right back to him. "I don't want this. I don't want you here."

"It's going to be all right," he says, attempting to calm me, that placating tone in his voice making me even angrier.

"Well, it's not now, and you need to get the fuck out," I say and seethe. I fold my arms across my chest as I look him in the eyes and tell him again. "I need space, and that means you're leaving." This townhouse is in both our names, I'm more than aware of that and he could easily bring that up. He has a right to be here and part of me wishes he would fight me on that, but he doesn't. He stares at the ground for a moment, his broad shoulders rising slowly with each heavy breath. My body shakes as he snatches his keys off the counter and leaves, slamming the door behind him.

I try to convince myself as I move to the counter, bracing my hot palms on the cold granite and focusing on breathing. This is the worst it's ever been between us.

I know it's the end of us. I can feel it deep down in my bones. Shattering my core.

Out of the need to move, to do something and just go through the motions, I reach for the bag on the counter.

It's a mistake. Inside is a bottle of coffee creamer.

It's so stupid that something like this could shred me. That it can make me fall to the floor. That it can make me feel like I've made the worst decision of my life.

That it makes me feel like I'm alone. And that it's my fault for pushing Evan away.

Chapter 10

Evan

It happened so slowly,
So slowly I couldn't see.
She ruined me, damned me,
And brought me to my knees.
I can't deny there was only one,
Only her for me.
One true love is a lie,
But with her, it has to be.

It's odd how love was there right from the start and I didn't even know it. Hindsight is twenty-twenty; I've made enough mistakes to know that. It doesn't explain how I couldn't see how obvious it was, right from the first night. Everything I did and said was different, everything I wanted changed.

My old bedroom in my father's house reminds me of all the times I spent here, but more than anything it reminds me of the last time I was in here. When I was crying like a bitch on my bed, burying my head into the pillow and refusing to accept that my mother was dying.

The red plaid flannel sheets are tucked in tight. It feels like this room's been frozen in time since I was here last. Kat fixed the sheets the same way when she made the bed the next morning. She held me all night. She let me cry and didn't tell me to stop or tell me to do anything at all. She just loved me. Freely and for no good reason.

I think she loved me from the very beginning, though. Looking back on it all, I know I had to have loved her right from the moment she stepped out of that car. The door shut with a click and my heart was finally in motion.

I remember that first date we had a few days after we met. I could still feel the beat of the heavy music in the club pumping through my veins as I opened the door to my apartment on the edge of Brooklyn. I glanced over my shoulder to take a peek at her, knowing the alcohol was wearing off and what I wanted was more than obvious. Part of me expected her to back out of coming upstairs.

I could tell she was surprised by how nice my place was. Maybe I can credit her curiosity for why she gathered up the nerve to follow my lead. There was a lot of remodeling going on in the city and I spent my money wisely, always have.

Investing in properties is what my father did when he had the chance. I learned from him, but did it on a much larger scale.

The second the door closed, my hands were all over her just like they had been in the taxi and in the club. We were drawn toward each other.

That's why I think it was love. Lust is one thing. It comes and goes. The moment you're filled and satisfied, disinterest takes its place. But that's never been the case for us. There was always more. Even as we grew apart, it only made what could be that much more tempting.

I turn the lights off in my bedroom as a distant siren drowns out the silence of the room and headlights from a passing car leave stripes of light moving through the small space.

Again, I remember what we used to have. Who we used to be. The first night we spent together is all I can think about. The day she ruined me forever. And I didn't even know it was happening.

She wrapped those sweet lips of hers around my dick before I could stop her. We'd only just gotten inside and I was planning on moving a little slower. I would've skipped the foreplay and gone straight for what I wanted if I didn't think she'd appreciate taking my time. When she dropped to her knees in front of me, taking me by surprise, I wasn't going to tell her no.

I was paralyzed as she dug her fingers into my thighs and sucked her way down my length. Her cheeks hollowed as she moaned and I swear I almost came just from the sight of her.

My balls tightened as she pulled back, letting my dick pop out of her mouth and then licking the tip. Her tongue slid up my slit as she worked my shaft and then did it again. The sight of her on her knees and practically worshipping my cock is something I can never forget. It was the shock mostly, I think. A woman who was already too good for me. A woman who was probably slumming it, was on her knees devouring me and loving every second of it.

My fingers speared through her hair as I closed my eyes and let myself enjoy it. Only for a moment, though. I wanted more of her and I was sure I only had the night.

Time moved so slowly as I savored each second of her, wanting more and knowing I could have it, but not ready for it to end.

She stared up at me, licking her lips and shaking her head when I tugged on her to come up and stop. Her lips were already swollen as she panted and then leaned forward. Ignoring me and taking what she wanted.

I watched as she closed her eyes and pushed me all the way to the back of her throat, forcing me to groan from deep in my chest. My dick twitches remembering how her mouth felt like heaven. I fisted my hand in her hair and pulled her off of me; it was fucking torture, wanting what she was giving me, but knowing I'd need more.

"Strip down," I groaned out, my head leaned back and my eyes closed. As if I had any control at all over her.

She shook her head again and I couldn't believe the plea that slipped from her lips.

"I want you to come in my mouth." She said it so simply, although breathlessly with her chest rising and falling, but full of truth. Her voice was laced with desire, but it was the way her shoulders rose and fell with her heavy breathing and the way she scooted closer to me, eager and begging for more that convinced me.

I could never say no to Kat. She doesn't ask for a damn thing. Never has, and I've wished she would. I'd give her the world if I could. But that night there was no fucking way I was going to deny her that.

I'm a selfish man, after all.

I slipped my hand around the back of her head as my toes curled. I was almost embarrassed by how quickly she got me off.

She didn't stop swallowing until I was spent and even then, she bobbed lightly on my dick and sucked like she wanted more. My greedy little sex kitten.

After she was done with me, when I'd pulled my pants up and stared down at her, the atmosphere changed.

"I don't have sex on the first date," she stated shyly, wiping her lips. A blush rose to her cheeks as she slowly stood up, trying to keep her balance by gripping onto my arm. She was hesitant, embarrassed maybe. I think it was vulnerability. I think she was afraid I'd be done. *She was afraid it was only lust.*

"Oh yeah?" I responded, still trying to catch my breath

and get a sense of who this girl was. "So what's this then?"

When I looked in her eyes, I knew what the real reason was. She thought I'd be done with her if I got her in bed.

More importantly, it meant she wanted to keep me.

The cockiness at that realization has never felt so good.

She wanted more and all the same, she was terrified to have me. Maybe scared she couldn't keep me, or scared to keep me. I still can't tell which was the motivating factor.

The thought made my still-hard dick even harder. And I stroked myself once and then again until she noticed. A smirk lifted up my lips as I saw her eyes widen.

"What if I want you? What if I want to take care of you now?" I asked her, taking a step forward and forcing her back. Her knees hit the bed and she nearly collapsed, the heat growing between us and nearly suffocating me.

I kissed my way down her neck, letting the heat between us climb higher and higher.

"Not just yet," I said as I stroked my dick again, feeling it turn hard as steel again already. "Let me taste you," I whispered.

Her gorgeous eyes peeked up at me through her thick lashes.

"Take it easy on me, will you?" Her words were playful, again feigning a strength that wasn't quite there. She was exposed and weak for me. Both of us knew it, only she was pretending she wasn't.

It's something that made me crave her more.

"Sure," I whispered in her ear as I pushed her onto the

bed. But I never had any intention of holding back when it came to her.

I fucked her as hard as I could into that mattress. I buried myself inside her and held off as long as possible, taking her higher and higher each time until she was holding on to me for her life. Her nails scratched and dug into my skin as she screamed out my name.

I destroyed her the best way I could. And I've never been more satisfied of anything else in my life.

Kat's an emotional woman. I didn't see it at first, but that night, our first night, I got my first taste of it. I could practically hear her tell me she loved me. If nothing else, I know she loved what I did to her.

I wanted to hear her tell me those words so badly. More than anything else, I wanted *this* woman to admit it. She fell in love with me that first night.

I was desperate for it.

I didn't realize that night that the look in her eyes was exactly what I felt too. Desperate to keep her, but knowing it was never supposed to happen.

I turn on my heels, facing the door as the sound of someone coming up the stairs brings me back to today. Six years later, that night is just a distant memory.

The door to my bedroom opens wide, creaking as it does and revealing my father. I haven't seen him like this in a long damn time.

His hair's been gray for a while, but it's just a bit too long and thinner. With the deep wrinkles around his eyes and only wearing a T-shirt and flannel pants, he looks older and frailer than I remember. Beaten down. Just a few years can change everything. Has it been that long since I really looked at him?

"You getting comfortable in here?" Pops asks me as he walks in and takes a look at the dresser. He runs a hand along it and then makes a face as he turns his hand over and sees the dust there. As he wipes his hand on the flannel pajamas he adds, "It's about time you came back to clean your room."

A rough chuckle barely makes its way up my chest.

"When are you moving out of this place?" I ask him jokingly.

"When I'm dead and gone," my father answers me the same way he has for years now. Ever since Ma passed, I've wanted him to move. He won't, though, and I can't blame him.

"Good thing I'm not in a nursing home. Don't think you'd like to crash there, would you?"

I give him a tight smile, feeling nothing but shame. I run my hand through my hair searching for some sort of an explanation, but I can't lie to my father and I don't want to tell him the truth. So I don't say anything and stare past him instead.

The silence is thick between us until he speaks, glancing around the room rather than looking at me.

"I messed up before with your mother, you know. She kicked me out. I thought it was over." My father flicks on the light and stalks slowly toward the bed, ignoring the fact that

I just wanted to pass out and try to sleep. As if I'd be able to in this room.

"I was younger than you, though. By the time I was your age, we'd had you. I'd settled down and stopped being stupid."

"What'd you do?" I ask my father out of genuine curiosity. I'd never seen anything but love from my parents. They never fought in front of me and the one time I came home early, catching them in the heat of a fight, they stopped immediately.

Later that night, when I was sitting in front of the TV, cross-legged and way too close, all I could hear was him apologizing in the kitchen. It'd been quiet all afternoon and night.

"I don't want you to go to bed mad at me," I heard him tell her.

It was the only fight I'd ever witnessed and I remember being scared that he'd done something that Ma wasn't going to forgive.

But she did. I never asked back then, and I'm sure if I did he wouldn't remember. This fight he's talking about obviously isn't that.

"What do you think I did?" he answers me. "We were young and stupid and had a bad fight over money or something. I got drunk, kissed a girl at a bar ... went back to her place. I felt like shit about it and she smacked me right across the face too." He smirks at the memory. "She beat the hell out of me. Kicked me out." The smile falls and he shakes his head as he adds, "I deserved it."

"I can't imagine you ever doing that."

"I loved your mother. I was angry at her over something stupid, I can't even remember what."

The silence stretches between us again as he struggles to come up with what to say next. "I proposed to her a few months after we got back together." A huff of a laugh leaves him and he adds, "God rest her soul," as he twists the wedding band around his ring finger. He's never taken it off. For the same reason he'll never leave this house.

He still needs her. Even if it's just the memory of her.

"The point is, we all make mistakes," he says and then squares his shoulders at me, raising both of his hands and shaking them, "when we're young and allowed to be stupid."

"I'm not that old," I tell him half-heartedly, trying to play it all off. I know what he's getting at, but I don't need to be lectured. I'm well aware of how stupid I've been. He's the one who has no idea how badly I've fucked up. "I'll fix it, Pops."

The silence drags on again and all I can think about is every position I've put myself in where not being faithful to my wife would have been the easy thing to do. I focus on that truth and not the night that still haunts me.

"What are you doing, Evan?" my father asks as I dump my bag on the bed. "You've fucked up more than you should have. You're too old to be carrying on like this."

My initial reaction is to bite back that he's wrong. That he has no idea what's going on. But it wouldn't matter.

I nod my head and let the strap from the bag fall off my shoulder. "Yeah, I know."

"You need to make this right," he tells me, holding my gaze and pointing a finger at me.

I swallow thickly, knowing he's right. But I haven't got a clue how to make this better. I can't take back what's been done.

I'm fucked.

"Yeah, I know."

Chapter 11

Kat

Just get it over with,
Tell me that we're done.
Leave me to this madness,
I accept that you have won.

You've broken me to pieces,
Left me numb and blind.
Made me only yours—
I've completely lost my mind.

"I need a distraction, that's what I need." I speak the words on my mind without realizing it. It gets the attention of both Maddie and Jules and that's when I realize I've said anything at all. Cue swallowing down another sip of wine.

We've been here in Jules's house helping her unpack for at least two hours now, and everyone's been kind enough to not only *not* ask about what's going on between Evan and me, but to not treat me like I'm some wounded animal either.

That's what friends are for, although the girls do seem to be walking on eggshells around me. I'm grateful, but I need to talk and have someone sift through this mess and give me a straight answer as to what I should do.

I roll my eyes at the thought. I'm a grown woman. I should know what to do and make the decision with certainty. But I've never felt so uncertain in my life.

"A distraction?" Jules questions, a little more pep in her tone than she's had all night.

"That makes sense," Maddie says and nods her head as she takes out a picture frame, wrapped in thick brown packing paper. She's careful with it as she removes the wrapping and exposes the pristine silver frame. "Distractions are a good thing," she adds with a small nod. "Sometimes."

I don't know what photo is already nestled inside of the frame, but whatever it is, it makes her smile. I can only imagine it's a wedding photo ... I lift the glass to my lips again.

"I can't go home to the townhouse with all his things and our things and every reminder of everything..." Pausing to take in a lungful of air, I try to steady myself then add, "Let alone go to sleep in the same bed we've had together for forever."

I stare at the artwork centered over Julia's fireplace as I talk.

The crinkling of the packaging paper is all the response I get from the other side of the expansive room. It's so loud that I'm not sure anyone but Maddie even heard me. We've been working in relative silence save for the soft sound of music flowing from the kitchen behind us.

"We should go on a girls' trip," I offer up and look over my shoulder at Maddie. I shift in my seat and wait for her to meet my gaze.

"Hell yeah," she answers without hesitation. "What does the newlywed think?" Maddie asks and instantly Jules brightens.

She shrugs as if the word *newlywed* didn't make her day and puts the attention back on me as she says, "I'm happy to do whatever you want, Kat." I hate that Jules is holding back. Every response from her tonight seems muted. She's happy and she knows I'm not. She's a newlywed and my marriage is falling apart.

I get it, but she should be happy. She doesn't have to hold back her joy because I'm falling apart.

"You're glowing," I tell her and wait for a response to the compliment, feeling guilty that I haven't said it sooner. My chest feels tight and I shift into a cross-legged position on the plush carpet as I grab a plastic bottle of water, drinking it down slowly even though it's room temperature now. The sweeping room of this new build is ridiculous. The entire house still smells of fresh paint. I can imagine they spent several million on it and the movers did most of the work carrying in all the heavy furniture. Jules didn't trust them with these boxes, though.

Maddie quirks an eyebrow. "You already make a baby?" she asks Jules, her tone devious. I can't help that my brow raises comically.

"Oh my God, Jules, are you pregnant?" I pile on and Maddie snickers as Jules pulls her tawny hair back and rolls her eyes.

"Shut up," Jules says playfully and then goes to the granite counter behind us and makes a show of drinking from her glass of wine. Her simple yet chic rose dress flutters as she waves her glass in the air. She's the epitome of an upper-class socialite.

We exchange amused looks, waiting for her to reply with a straight yes or no.

"Not yet," Jules finally answers.

"Yet!" Maddie practically shrieks. "First comes love, then comes marriage—"

"Then comes a new home and a fresh start," Jules says, cutting her off and Sue laughs from her spot in the corner of the living room where she's been silent all night. Something's definitely gotten to Sue too.

Although maybe it's me, maybe I'm why everyone seems off.

"House first, then the baby," Jules states and then switches the song playing to something more upbeat and less sad. I agree with that decision wholeheartedly.

"Love your house," Sue comments, not bothering to bring

up the idea of a child. "Or is it technically a mansion?" she half jokes.

It's grand and spacious and much more like Jules's style than her new husband Mason's previous home. She got a deal on this property and the amount of space is making me regret buying a place so close to the park. It reminds me how tiny our townhouse is. At least compared to this. Location is everything and we paid handsomely for our little place.

This is also a family home, and I live in a townhouse that's not meant for anything more than two people ... potentially one child, but it would be cramped. I force my lips to stay in place and swallow down the frown and all the feelings threatening to come up.

Full circle I go, all day long. My thoughts always come back to Evan and what we had and everything we could still have.

With a bitter sigh I hope no one heard, I finish my water and get up to grab another drink, shimmying past the three opened boxes and paper sitting on the floor. I made this decision. I need to own up to it and deal with the consequences.

"I'm not sure I can do this girls' trip," Sue says seemingly out of nowhere. I'd nearly forgotten about the mention of a trip. I guess that's how much it means to me.

"It's just that work ..." she adds and then pauses to chew the inside of her cheek. She braces herself on a polished wingback chair before rising and picking up her wineglass.

"I've got a new boss and he's a dick with a capital D. There's no way he's going to give me time off."

"It's not really his position to give it to you," Maddie says skeptically. "Like, you *earn* your days. And we haven't even set a date yet." The aggressiveness in Maddie's voice catches me off guard.

Sue stands, an empty glass in hand, meeting me at the small sink filled with ice and bottles of rosé and cabernet. With a glass of wine in her right hand and a ball of packaging paper in her left, she strides past a very young and not at all familiar with the corporate world Maddie, and responds with certainty, "He'll give me shit."

"So fuck him," Maddie says, a little anger coming out. She doesn't usually get worked up, so I'm taken aback. Everyone is off today ... there must be something in the air.

"It's fine, it was just a thought," I say and try to smooth the tension flowing between the two of them. "You okay?" I direct my question at Maddie, who doesn't seem to notice it's for her, picking up her wineglass and throwing it back.

"I don't want to set a bad precedent," Sue states staring directly at Maddie, who refuses to look back at Suzette.

My gaze moves between the two of them and I'm only distracted by the loud clap behind me from Jules. "Who wants some charcuterie?" Jules says and we all turn slowly to see her lifting a tray of cut meats and cheese as if it's the peace treaty between us.

Sue has the decency to laugh and the small moment of tension is immediately diffused.

I feel odd sitting in this room all of a sudden. Looking around the room, I'm surrounded by friends, but I feel alone. I take another sip of water. It's all in my head, I'm more than aware of that, but it doesn't change how I feel.

"Have you slept with him?" Jules regards me as she grabs a contraption from one of her drawers that she uses to uncork the wine bottles. The kitchen is all white. White cabinets and a sleek white countertop. The only color is in the ebony floorboards. It's luxurious and would be fitting for an editorial photoshoot. Which I promptly told her the moment I stepped foot in this place. I am her agent after all.

"Who with who?" Maddie asks for clarification with a sly smile on her face. "Is Sue sleeping with her boss?" Her question makes Suzette tense and stare back at Maddie with daggers. But Maddie's oblivious. The two of them should have their own show. If it was up to me, they would and the ratings would be through the roof. Maddie would probably go for it, Sue would never.

"Kat," Jules answers and her tone is casual, not sympathetic or pushy, no motive apparent. "Have you slept with Evan since it all happened?" she asks again, but more directly and pops the cork from the bottle.

It fizzes as my face heats, knowing the other two women are looking at me, but I wait for Jules. The second she raises her eyes to mine, although it was only meant to be a glance, I nod my head.

I anticipate the scoff of disdain from Sue, the tilted head with a sympathetic look from Maddie, but I don't know what to expect from Jules.

She shrugs her shoulders, the soft pink fabric slipping down and making her look that much thinner, that much more beautiful. "Was it any good?" she asks and lifts the glass to her lips. It's dark red wine, the same color she wears on her lips. It's one thing I like about Jules; she's nothing if not consistent.

Rolling my eyes, I wipe my face with my hand. It's always good with Evan. "It was a mistake," I tell her instead. My dismal tone immediately changes the mood and frustration flows through me.

"People make mistakes," Jules says low, so low I almost didn't hear her. And then she looks at me and adds, "It happens." She sounds so sad and I can't help but to wonder what's going on with her. For just a moment, a short glimpse, there's something there other than the perfect façade she always carries. But the moment she registers that I can see it, the crack in her demeanor, she straightens her shoulders and takes in a heavy breath.

Silence passes and the only thing that can be heard is the rustling of paper as Maddie unwraps something. Staring down into the newly poured glass of wine I realize I've never felt so alone and unwelcomed. It's not them, it's me and my head, I know it is. "I just don't know what to do," I say, speaking to all of them or none of them, it doesn't matter, I just needed to say it. "We slept together and I think it was a mistake ... Because I kicked him out the next morning." A groan leaves me, nearly comical, as I take a small sip but it's not satisfying. Not nearly large enough either.

"You don't need to decide right now," Jules says easily. "There's a lot to consider and talk about." She nods her head as she talks, almost like she's talking to herself.

"The thing is ... I don't know what I want, but I know he'll convince me to stay with him."

"Men have a way with words," Sue chimes in, agreeing with me, and tips her glass in an air-cheers with me. "It's called lying."

I huff in agreement, opting for my water instead of more wine, as I watch Sue saunter over to the tray of cheese.

"I mean ... not that he lied ... he's just ..." Sue says softly and then clears her throat to add with a touch of sympathy, "I keep letting my shitty experience color my opinion. Sorry," she says, looking me in the eyes. The sincerity there kills me.

"It's fine. It's called experience."

"So you're indecisive, and that makes sense. You're married. You love him. But you're hurt." Maddie cuts through all the silence and unease like it's so simple and easy to comprehend. But it's not. There's a raging war of emotions inside of me. I don't know that I can trust my husband, and that alone is enough to end it and what pushed me to kick him out this morning.

Rather than confess about my lack of trust, I offer a partial truth. "I slept with him last night and then kicked him out this morning." I shake my head realizing how awful that sounds, how crazy it seems.

"Sounds like a divorce to me," Sue says and then fills her glass again. "I did it for years, Kat. Years of back and forth. Forgiving but not forgetting." Her slender fingers play on the stem of the glass. "Wish I had those years back."

The need to defend Evan overrides my common sense. "I don't know what I did that pushed him away." Even as I say the words, I know that's not true. I let distance grow between us. I ignored him in favor of my career.

"Nothing, it's not you. It's not your fault." Sue's words are hard, with no negotiation allowed. So I don't correct her.

Maddie adds in, ever comforting, "It's not your fault in the least. Don't let him make you feel that way."

They don't understand. They just don't get it.

"What if—"

Sue cuts me off to say, "If you want to sleep with him, do it. Want to kick him out, do it. Want to hurl something at his head … maybe don't because that's assault." Her joke forces a bark of a laugh from me and a snicker from Jules. Her glass setting down on the counter offers a clink and she adds, "Yes please, for the love of all things holy don't make us come bail you out."

"You would, though," I say and cock a brow, knowing any of the three of these women would bail me out in a heartbeat.

"It's whatever you want," Maddie continues and Jules and Sue both nod. "You can be friends with benefits if that's what you want, fuck buddies, you can use him for revenge sex. I don't think any of us have any answers other than we're here for you." She side-eyes Sue and adds, "Although Sue is cockblocking our girls' trip."

"Oh my Lord, someone ... get her," Sue groans and Jules and I laugh while Maddie purses her lips and tosses a balled-up bit of paper at Sue's back. It doesn't reach, but the comic relief helps to calm all the nerves I've been feeling. Most of them, anyway. There's still a little flutter in the pit of my stomach.

"We'll plan a girls' trip," Jules states as if it's a fact. "It just might be a bit difficult, but we will make this happen and it'll be great for you to get out."

"I think it will be fun, and I'll figure out how to make it work," Sue says all the while staring at Maddie who finally smiles.

"Yes. Girls' trip and fuck or dump whomever we want ... Except Jules. Because she might be pregnant."

I nearly choke on my wine at that thought.

Chapter 12

Evan

I tried it. I swear I tried to give her space.

Kat says that's what she needs, but I know it's not. This plan of hers isn't what she needs and it's sure as hell not what I want.

She needs me. Period. She needs me to be there and that's where I've failed. Not just in the last few weeks. For years, I chose a lifestyle that forced us apart.

I can fix this, but not by running to Pops and leaving her all alone with nothing but this city whispering in her ear.

My arm stiffens as I slide the key into the lock to our townhouse. My heart doesn't beat until it turns, proving she didn't change the locks. I let out a breath I didn't know I was still holding and push it open. I'm prepared with what I need to say. Prepared to hold my ground and not take no for an answer.

But it only takes one step inside of our living room for all of it to slip away from me.

Kat looks so tired, so worn out propped up in the corner of the sofa with her laptop sitting to the left of her, but the screen's black. She has a cup of coffee in her hands as well as bags under her eyes. She turns to me slowly, wiping the sleep from her eyes and adjusting herself slightly. With the gentle protest of the sofa, I shut the door behind me.

"What are you doing here?" she asks me, still seated with her legs tucked underneath her on the sofa. I'm stunned for a moment because she's so fucking beautiful, even in this state. My body's drawn to her. If it were another time, I'd go to the sofa, push the laptop off and lie down, making her take a break. I'd kiss her until her body writhed against mine.

And she'd let me. She'd let me make her relax. At least she would have a year ago.

"This is my house." I try not to say the words too firmly. "Our house," I correct myself and swallow before continuing and taking a single step closer to her. "I worked my ass off—"

"Then I'll move out," Kat quickly states matter-of-factly, but the pain is barely disguised. She seems to snap out of whatever daze had her captive before I came in here.

"I don't want you to move out. We don't need this." I emphasize my words.

"I asked for time and space because I don't know what to do, Evan. You aren't giving me any options without telling me what happened."

"You want to know?" I look her in the eyes, feeling my blood pulse harder in my veins.

"Are you going to tell me the truth?" she asks me in a cracked whisper. "All of it?"

All of it? I have to break her gaze. I can't. I can't confess everything. I'd lose her forever.

The second I break eye contact, she scoffs. "You're so full of shit. Why are you doing this to me?" she asks me, although it's rhetorical. There's a loathing in her tone but more than that it's pain.

Why am I doing this to her? If it was only so easy as *doing* something. There's nothing I can do.

"I didn't come home to fight."

"Neither did I ... but here we are," she retorts, taking in a shuddering breath. "I asked for time, Evan."

Tossing my keys on the coffee table, I make my way into the living room and sit across from her in the armchair. I'm not foolish enough to think she'd let me sit close enough to touch her. Even as I sit here, feet away, she bends her legs in closer and pushes the laptop to the side. Like she's ready to run at a moment's notice.

Time slips by as I lean back, letting a long exhale take up some of it. "I just want to be home with you while this blows over."

"Blows over?" I don't know how she can make a whisper seem hysterical. I'm not good with words. I never have been, but I wish I had the wisdom to say the right thing right now.

"Maybe this is the moment," she states with a sad smile on her beautiful face.

"The moment?"

"The moment that changes everything for the rest of my life. I've been wondering exactly what moment it was, but thought maybe it hasn't happened yet."

Her words settle deep in my very core and a tingling runs through my fingers up my arms. Slow, yet all-consuming. Her face changes from the sarcastic disappointment that she had when she said the words. As if only just now realizing the magnitude of them herself.

"We can go back. I promise," I tell her softly, raising my hands just slightly, but the fear of losing her keeps my blood cold and my motions subtle.

"It's called separating for a reason," she says, whispering her response. As if what we had the other night meant nothing. As if there's no reason for us to be together. Maybe she really doesn't love me anymore. The fissure in my chest deepens, feeling like it's cracked wide open.

"We're not separated."

"Yes we are."

"We didn't decide to do that," I answer her. "You were angry."

"Rightfully so," she spits back.

"I told you it's not true," I plead with her as I stare deep into her eyes. I watch as they gloss over and her lower lip trembles. "Just ..." I swallow thickly, the lump growing in the back of my throat suffocating any plea I have for her. *Just love me. Just forgive me.*

I turn away from her for a moment, not able to voice what I'm feeling. I lean forward in the chair, and it creaks as I rest my weight in it. Kat starts to get up in response.

"I don't want to fight," I remind her.

"I don't want this, Evan. I didn't ask for this," she says, raising her voice for the second part, the anger coming back. She stops moving, though, and I can tell she's losing the will to fight. It's by the way her lips are parted just so, and her breathing is quicker and she has that little crease in the center of her forehead.

"I don't know what to do or say, or what to think. I feel crazy." She stares at me wide eyed, her voice sounding hoarse. "Do you understand what that's like? To be so stupid? To know I'm being stupid and setting myself up for you to hurt me again."

"I won't hurt you—" The truth rushes out of me in a single breath, but she doesn't let me finish.

"But you did," she says, cutting me off and rocking forward just slightly as she points out the obvious. "And you won't even tell me why." Her shoulders shudder, but she doesn't cry, she holds her ground.

"I don't want to lose you, Kat," I manage to speak and

peek up to look at her. I'm such a piece of shit. "I just want you. It's the honest to God truth. I just want you."

"I want you to quit," she tells me and rocks on her feet to stand. She nods her head and visibly swallows. "You need to quit." She stares at me, her emerald eyes pleading. Her body's still, like she's not breathing. Just waiting.

"It's not that easy," I say and God I wish she knew. I want to tell her everything, but I can't risk it. I can't leave right now. I just need time.

"It is that easy; you quit or leave." I stare into her eyes that swirl with nothing but raw vulnerability, and hesitate.

"You're giving me an ultimatum?" Even as I ask her, I know that's what she's doing.

She has no idea.

"I just need time." I need her to just give me time. As soon as I'm out of this, I can do whatever she wants.

But not right now.

I can feel her slipping away. Every second that passes where I don't tell her, she's turning colder toward me. But she can't know. No one can.

My lips part and I can feel my lungs still. The words are right there. Begging me, and desperate for her to hear. I need her more than anything.

"Kat." I say her name but it's so much more. It's me begging for her to love me blindly, to trust that I love her and that I'd never do anything to hurt her.

I can't. I can't risk losing her, and I won't do it.

My mouth closes and I turn away from her, running my hand over my face.

"Get out," Kat states and her voice hitches at the end. I turn to see her cover her face.

The next bit happens so fast. It's a blur as I close the distance between us. It only takes three steps, but by the time my arms wrap around her, she's pushing me away. Her hands slam into my chest. She tries to knock me back, but only manages to throw herself off-balance instead.

I grip her hips to steady her, but she slaps me. Hard across the face and the sting catches me by surprise.

I flex my jaw as she screams at me to get out. Her body's shaking. The sinful mix of hatred and betrayal ring in the air between us.

How the hell did I let this happen?

"Do you really want me out?" I ask her, genuinely not knowing anymore. I don't know at what point I lost her completely. There's only so many times I can ask her to give me everything while I hold back.

I guess I should be more surprised it hasn't happened sooner.

Rubbing my jaw as I take a step back, I give her the only bit of space I'm willing to offer. "I know you still love me," I tell her and watch as she rips her eyes from me. Her face is blotchy and red and her breathing is frantic.

But she calms as she stands there not able to answer me.

That's all I needed. Just a little bit. *Please, Kat. Just hold on a little while longer.*

"Just tell me the truth," she begs me and I wish I could. I feel my throat tighten and my body tense. My hands clench as I swallow.

"I didn't sleep with her." I answer without wasting a second and even I don't believe my words. But it's not what she thinks. I wish I could tell her, but the moment she finds out, everything will be at risk.

"Why don't I believe you?" she says and I don't have the decency to answer.

"I swear, Kat."

"So you've never slept with her?" she asks me and I know it's over. Her expression changes and her eyes darken when the silence stretches too long. So many secrets have built up. Too many to hide. She was never supposed to know. "Since we've been married," I start to say, knowing I'm toeing the line of truth, "I've never slept with anyone. Never kissed anyone but you." I look her in the eyes so she can see it's the truth. "The day I put that ring on your finger, it was only you."

"Then why put me through this?" she asks me with tears in her eyes. "And what were you doing?" I struggle to keep my breathing calm as the questions start piling up. "What were you doing with her in that hotel if you weren't sleeping with her."

I lick my dry lips and take a step forward. "Things got out of hand."

"Why were you with her?" Kat presses and I know she wants an answer right now.

"Because it's what I had to do," I say, telling her the truth with my eyes closed.

"What you had to do? You had to go to her hotel at three in the morning?" I can't look at her as I nod my head. "And you couldn't tell me this before?" I nod my head again.

"You tell me everything right now, or you leave."

"Another ultimatum?" The words drip with disdain.

"Don't talk to me like that," she says. Her tone is dismissive and I can hear her resolve harden.

"It's better if you didn't know everything," I answer gently yet firmly just the same.

"Are you serious right now? You're throwing away our marriage over her? Over your job?"

"Kat, just—" I start to say, but she cuts me off.

"Fuck you," she sneers then yells, "I said get out."

"I'm not leaving," I tell her firmly, staring back at her, even as she turns her back to me.

"It doesn't matter, the weekend's coming," she says beneath her breath as she leaves me.

I keep my feet planted as she stomps up the stairs and I wait for more. I wait for her to push me out, to yell at me, to demand more from me. I'm ready to fight, ready for war with her to keep her. But that's not what I get.

She gives me back exactly what I gave her. *Nothing.*

Chapter 13

Kat

F our manuscripts to go through this weekend.

Four authors waiting to hear back from me.

I doubt I'll be able to focus enough to comprehend a full page. I've been reading the same paragraph over and over and not a damn sentence is staying with me.

It doesn't matter, though. None of this really does.

All that matters is that I stay in this office for as long as Evan's here. He's like a ghost in this house. A ghost of his former self.

So I do what I've always done, I bury myself in work. That was the plan anyway, but now I can't focus on anything but the sounds of him moving through the house.

He walks by the door every few hours, making the floor groan, and I know he wants to open it, wants me to talk to him. All I can hear is him saying it'd be better if I didn't know. To hell with that.

I'm not going to give him all of me when he can't be bothered to do the same. There is nothing more important than us. Not a single thing that should come between us; yet it feels like he's got plenty in the space between my heart and his.

So we're at a standstill, him refusing to leave and me refusing to blindly forgive.

His voice plays in my head over and over again, telling me it's only ever been me. I want to believe it. It's everything I've been praying for him to say.

But then what is he hiding?

My eyes flicker to the screen as my nails tap on the pale blue ceramic mug next to my laptop. *Tick, tick, tick.* I read the line over and over: *Love is a stubborn heart.*

Magdalene, the editor, highlighted the line. She thinks it's beautiful and she wants repetition of the metaphor throughout the book.

Love is a stubborn heart.

Is it, though? My forehead scrunches as I think back to the story in the manuscript. The tale about a modern-day Romeo and Juliet. Two families who hated each other and their children who wanted nothing more than to run away together. It's not a tragedy but it doesn't have a happily ever after either. It's too realistic.

If love really was that stubborn, wouldn't they have been together in the end?

Maybe it wasn't really love.

Or maybe love just wasn't enough.

I don't know that I agree that love is stubborn. I suppose it is, but more than that, it's stealthy and lethal. I nod my head at the thought.

Love is deadly.

Rolling my eyes. I push the laptop away. My comments don't belong on this manuscript right now.

I don't know the very moment I fell in love with Evan. It felt like I was counting the days until it would be over, and then one day, I simply decided on forever. Just like that, a snap of my fingers. Slow, so slow and resistant, and then in an instant, I was his and he was mine. And that's how it was going to be forever.

I smile at the thought and try to focus on the lines staring back at me from the computer. I try to read the words, but I keep glancing at the wall behind me. At a photo of the first night he took me to meet his parents. It was after I'd decided on forever.

I'd never felt that kind of fear before. The fear of rejection. Not like I did that night and I know why: it's because I'd never put my heart out there for anyone to take.

I was very much aware that Evan had every piece of me.

Unless he didn't want me. In which case, I'd be broken and I didn't know how I'd recover.

The thought consumed me the night he brought me to his family home. I was sure his family wouldn't like me. It'd been so long since I'd been with a family for dinner. I used to go to my friend Marissa's when I was in high school. But that's not the same. Not at all. It was also a rarity that I accepted Marissa's parents' offer for dinner.

When you lose your parents at fifteen, people tend to look at you as though they've never seen anything sadder. I'd rather be alone than deal with that.

So I was, until Evan. And he didn't come on his own, he had a family that "had to meet me."

My back rests against the desk chair as my gaze lingers on the photograph. I had it printed in black and white. It's the four of us on the sofa in his family home's living room. It's funny how I can see the colors of the sofa so clearly, the faded plaid, even though there isn't any color in the picture that hangs on my wall.

All four of us are smiling. His mother insisted on taking the photo. Just as she'd insisted he bring me that night.

It's only now that I can remember how Evan's father looked at her. I didn't think anything of it at the time, but that's because they hadn't told us that she was sick.

I guess in some ways it was the last photograph. If that isn't accepting someone into your family, I don't know what is.

I have to hold back the prick of tears as I think of her. I only met Marie a handful of times. The dinner was the second. The third was after she'd told Evan; she didn't have a choice, seeing as how she had to be hospitalized. The last time I saw her was at the funeral.

I may not know when I fell in love with him, but I think I know the moment he fell in love with me. The moment a part of his heart died and he needed something, or someone, to fill it. Maybe I got lucky that it was me. Or maybe it was a curse.

I roll my eyes, hating that I'm stuck in the past because I can't move ahead with the future.

Maybe we weren't really meant to be. Maybe it was never the type of love that's meant to keep people together. Just the type of love when you feel compelled to give someone compassion.

Are there types of love? I find myself leaving the question as a comment on the book and then deleting it.

If there are, then maybe Evan's love is the stubborn kind. He's not so stubborn that he'll stay this weekend, though. Come Friday he'll be gone again. Maybe it's a different kind of love then ...

It's only when I hear the bedroom door shut that I finally look back at the manuscript and email the editor back. I need more time before I can give feedback on any of these to the author and I'm ready to fall asleep in the corner chair, or any place I can where Evan will leave me alone.

I need more time for so much more. I need time and a clear head to move forward with my own life. I need someone to tell me I'm not walking away from the only man who will ever love me, but there's no email I can write for that unfortunate request.

Chapter 14

Evan

If I could focus on the hate and leave her all alone,
I'd be able to move forward, if only I had known.
I can't speak the truth, I don't want to make it real,
I can't stand what I've done or what it makes me feel.
Regret will settle in my chest and suffocate the day.
If only I could make it right, if only there was a way.

"It's good to see New York again," James says as I walk into his office on Greene Street in lower Manhattan.

Even as he speaks, he stares out the office window. It's an impressive eight-by-eight-foot picture window, making the view seem like it's not quite real.

I don't return his sentiment. I'm fucking miserable regardless of the scenery or location. I want to drop to my knees and confess everything to Kat. The weight of it all is burying me. I think she'd forgive me. I can see it in her eyes that she wants to accept anything I'm willing to divulge. I could tell her almost everything and I think she'd let me stay.

I'm too scared to do it, though, and bring her into this mess. If they find out she knows ... she just can't know. Not until I end things here at least. It's step one to getting my Kat back.

"It's crazy how you miss it, isn't it?" he continues as he turns to me. He's more relaxed than he was in London, although his suit is crisp and fresh from the dry cleaner. I close the door as he takes a seat at the desk, unbuttoning his dark gray jacket.

"Sorry you had to wait a minute, I was just getting this paperwork wrapped up." He leans back in his chair, loosening his slim navy tie and unfastening the top button of his crisp white dress shirt.

"Are we going to talk about it?" I ask, needing to get this shit off my chest. I kept quiet in London, but I can't anymore. It's been weeks. That must be enough time.

Is that how long it takes to get away with murder?

"Talk about what?" he questions and his voice is gravelly and low.

"Talk about the fact that the charges against Bruce are dropped?" I say then hold his cold gaze with one I hope informs him I have no time for bullshit and I'm out of patience.

He may have been relaxed before I sat down, but now he's

still. And silent. I let my eyes fall to the stack of papers on his desk, then drift to a small picture frame. It's a cube and matte black on all sides, and I have no idea who the woman in the picture is.

I absently pick it up, ignoring how his eyes bore into me, how his icy gaze heats as I let the question hang in the air, forcing him to answer.

The block is lighter than I thought it'd be and I don't recognize the broad with a closer look either. It's not his ex-wife, or his current girlfriend. Not that I thought Luna or whatever her name was, the fling of the month, would have a place in his office.

"My sister," James says, answering the unasked question. "A Christmas gift."

I nod my head once, putting the block back down and waiting for him to answer me.

"Bruce didn't *do* anything, so of course the charges didn't stick," James states in an eerily calm voice. "We knew he was innocent." James pulls out a drawer and shuffles something inside of it, but I can't see what. He doesn't elaborate or give any room to further the conversation that we should have.

"What's done is done, and there's nothing more to say."

"That's not what Sam told me. She told me she's scared." It's the only reason I let her get so close. She's terrified that the truth is going to come out. She helped me, so she'd go down with me.

"Whose fault is that?" James sneers.

"She's your wife," I say, pushing out the words through my clenched teeth.

"I don't have a wife," he answers me with a sly smile, as if he's clean of this mess. As if it's all on me. Deep down in my gut, I know it is.

"Ex then," I concede and add, "I didn't know the divorce had been finalized." He picks up a pen and taps it against the desk but doesn't take his eyes off me. It hasn't gone through yet, according to Samantha. All the money needs to be split one way or the other, and neither him nor Samantha, his ex-partner in this business and future ex-wife, wants to take less than the other.

"Either way, what's done is done and the two of you need to let it die."

"An innocent man—"

"Got off!" He looks me in the eyes as he leans forward and adds, "And a guilty man got away."

"We should have come forward."

"Should have, but you listened to a shady bitch. That's your problem, not mine."

My gaze falls to the desk as my fingers itch to form a fist. I called *him*. The number I dialed that night was to *his* office. I had no idea she'd be the one who answered.

"I panicked—" I start to say, but he cuts me off.

"Because you fucked up. And now I have to clean up your

mess and make sure you stay out of trouble."

"Is that what this is? You doing me a favor?" I ask sarcastically, letting the memory of that night fade. I can't quit while there's still an investigation. I can't bring more attention to myself or to the company. One of my clients dies and I get fired or quit shortly after? Yeah, that'll get the police's attention.

I wish I could tell Kat everything, but then she'd know she was married to a murderer. Even if it was just an accident. I'm a coward and I'll never be a man she deserves. But every day that goes by, I want to be more of the man I was the day before it all changed.

"I need time off," I state, fed up with the conversation. I imagine this isn't the first time something like this has happened and I sift through the memories of all the shit that's gone on behind the scenes for years. I never questioned anything, I never suspected a thing. Not until James brought me into the inner circle.

"No," James answers immediately with no negotiation in his voice.

"Then I quit," I tell him as my fingers dig into the chair. The only thing I can think about is Kat. She'll get over the fact I kept this from her. I know she will. It's not the first time I've kept a secret from her. We'll be okay as long as I'm through with this shit.

His thin lips twist into a half smile as he says, "Well, that can't happen." He looks at me with a calculated glint in his eyes. Like he's been waiting for this and he's ready for my rebuttal, eager for it even.

"Why not?" I question as my muscles coil. Even though I'm aware it could cause suspicion, I can do whatever the fuck I want. "I'm not going to work for this company anymore."

"That's not—"

"It's called quitting," I spit back at him. I don't need this job; I've got plenty of money in the bank and my investments, and Kat's career is finally stable. She bled money for years, but it's leveling out. We'll be all right financially and this is what she wants and what I need.

"You can't just quit."

"I can, and I am."

James's smile fades and he tilts his head to the side, an expression of the utmost sympathy on his weathered face. His deep brown eyes look darker as he picks up a folder on the left side of his desk. It wasn't hidden, but it's not labeled and it looks like all the rest.

My eyes follow his movement and my brow furrows until he opens it.

"The hotel had cameras. They're gone now, of course, but a few snapshots were taken. Some I think you'd find particularly interesting. Maybe enough so to stay."

I can imagine what they are before he flips the folder open. The eight-by-ten glossy photo paper shows the one thing that proves I lied. I'm walking into the hotel lobby I claimed I didn't enter. And I'm not alone. Standing right next to me is Tony. Only hours before he was found dead in the rec room of the hotel. The one reserved for our company and the division Bruce is the head of. The photograph of Tony and his bloodshot eyes takes me back to that night. To the moment I found him dead on the floor.

My limbs freeze in waves. Like the betrayal that moves through me.

"It's a security net on my end," James says and then closes the folder, pulling it off the desk and into his lap.

"So if I quit," I start to say, but instead I stop and stare ahead out of the window. I want to kill him. There's never been a time in my life when I've desired someone dead. But right now, it's all I want.

"Then I assume it's for less than moral reasons," James says, spelling it out for me. "I need to protect myself."

"That's bullshit," I tell him and my words are hard. My hands turn to fists as they tremble with the need to get this anger out.

"I know, trust me I know," James says. "And I don't like this any more than you do."

A sarcastic huff of a laugh leaves me. "Fuck off," I sneer at him.

I stand up from the office chair so quickly it nearly falls over. I grip it so tight I think I'll break it. Fuck, I want to break it. I can picture beating the piss out of him with the broken wood.

My body is hot, my mind in a daze of regret and sickness.

"I'm leaving," I barely speak as I turn my back to him and start to walk off.

"The fuck you are," he says.

My body whips around, tense and ready to let it all out. Every day it's been building and building, the tension winding tighter and the need to destroy something climbing higher and higher. I only took a few steps away, and with his words I'm right back across the desk, ready to do something stupid.

My body heats as my fist moves from the chair to the desk and I lean closer. He may not want to show it, but I see the fear in his eyes.

He should be scared. He's fucking with me. Threatening me. No one is going to take my wife from me. I won't allow it.

"I need to get away from this. From you."

I never should have listened to him and tried to cover it up. He set me up. He used that night to his advantage and I played right into his hand.

It takes everything in me not to reach across the desk and haul him up by his collar. To fist the fine cloth in my grip and spit in his face.

Pure rage and adrenaline pump through my blood.

"Careful now, Evan." James smiles as he says it, but I notice how he leans back. Both of us know he's scared. If I throw this punch, if I push, he could bring it all to light.

And then I'll lose her forever.

"I'm going home, and I'll let you know when I'm available again." *Never.* The word is whispered in the back of my head. I'm never returning to this office. I'm never doing another thing for this prick.

"You can't leave me. I'll ruin you," he practically whispers with nothing but hate. He says the words I already know.

"Ruin me then," I respond easily, looking into his dark eyes as I turn the doorknob and leave him behind me. On the surface I'm calm, but brewing just beneath my skin is nothing but chaos. Everything I've feared has finally come.

Proof I was there.

Proof I lied to the police.

I leave the office with the threat echoing in my head. I did this to myself, digging the hole deeper and deeper.

There's no way Kat will stay when it all goes down.

Chapter 15

Kat

Never trapped, never alone,
This city never sleeps.
Even in the daylight,
The sins are left to creep.
They tempt me and pull me,
And make me feel alive.
My mouth is dry, my body hot.
In temptation regrets will thrive.

My iPhone lights up as I push the top button to check the time again, and then again to look at the date. I'm anxious for this meeting; unusually so. Then again, I'm anxious all the time now.

Evan hasn't come home; he isn't talking to me. It's been

four days and each day I feel like I need to cave more and more. I didn't know how much I wanted him there until he was gone. I just need him back.

A huff leaves me and I shake my head at the thought. Breakups are always hard and that's what this is, so there's only one way to move on and that's to get it over with.

I don't want to be in our townhouse, but I have nowhere else to go.

An easy breath leaves me as I stand behind the only woman in line at Brew Madison and tilt my head to read the sign on the back wall. All the beverages they have to offer are written on a large chalkboard, and large bakery cases house all the treats they have available. From small pastries to toasted breakfast sandwiches, all lined up as if they're plastic replicas, even though I know they're freshly made and just simply that good.

I haven't had much of an appetite, but every sip of my coffee this morning made me nauseated, so a blueberry muffin top it is.

The brunette curls of the woman in front of me swing from side to side as she gives her order. I can't see her face, but I know she's young. From her bright red high heels and black leather jacket paired with white shorts a bit too short for fall, she's definitely a downtown girl.

I smile at the thought as she waits for her coffee: pumpkin spice.

I used to be like her. Stylish and in charge of my destiny.

New to the city and ready to tame it.

I thought I had.

A career and reputation in this publishing industry that I reached within only a few years. I'm an agent worth my weight now and everyone knows it. My name and brand have a meaning to them. The clients are coming in and I'm able to hire more reps and editors. It's the business I've always wanted. More than that, I'm married to a man who still drips of sex appeal and has an edge to him that is irresistible. We own our townhouse near Madison Square Garden. Even if it is small, it's the closest we could get. And it's New York, so location is *everything*.

And my closet ... the girl in front of me would kill for my closet. Not that she would know it based on how I'm dressed at the moment.

My name has a purpose and strength to it that made me proud. Evan and I were a powerhouse in the social scene. The couple everyone wanted to be. But envy comes with threats and in its nature, ruins. Rumors and gossip created a wedge between the two of us.

In the last few years, the highs of this world have crashed as my marriage slowly dissolved.

I let it. I spent my life not living it, wanting more and more from my work. Running as fast as I could, just to stay still while I ignored every other change in the world around me. How could I not have seen it deteriorating?

As the woman turns and I get a look at her cat eye makeup that's subtle enough to still be businesslike and red lips that match her heels, I remember that feeling that used to flow through me. The one that said I could conquer anything.

Yeah, I used to be like her. I still have the heels and even the stylish clothes, although I lean toward professional these days with my wardrobe and those shorts sure as heck don't lean that way.

"What can I get you?" the young man asks me from behind the counter. He's got to be in his early twenties at most. I catch a glimpse of his sleeve tattoo and it reminds me of Evan's tattoos for only a moment.

More thoughts of Evan. Everything reminds me of him.

"A chai and a blueberry muffin top," I answer him with a tight voice and clear my throat as I reach for my card in my wallet. It's a Kate Spade and the soft pink and white match the purse, but I'm only just now realizing that it looks a bit dingy. Not so much so that it's noticeably dirty. Just enough where it doesn't look so new anymore.

As I wait for my chai, I get a look at my reflection in the glass. I guess the same can be said about me. My fingers tease my hair at the roots, putting a little more volume there and I apply a coat of stain on my lips while I wait.

I wrap the belt around my shirt a little tighter, showing off my waist and lean to my right in the reflection.

I'm not done yet. There's still life in me. There's still that girl who wants more buried deep down inside. But what exactly she wants more of remains a question.

Evan, the silent answer, is obvious.

But instead the voice in my head whispers *love*.

Even if he can't give me everything, I know what I'm desperate for: to love and be loved.

The bells to the door chime as I accept my chai and muffin top. I silently pray that it's not Jacob so I can have a moment to try to shovel this down.

No such luck.

I smile broadly when I see him, hiding everything I was just thinking and focusing on my potential client and his career. I mentally tally up how much work we both need to do to get his branding both going in the right direction and noticed by the right market.

"Jacob," I greet him and his deep green, hazel eyes focus on me.

"Katerina, it's wonderful to finally have a one-on-one," he says as he steps over the welcome mat and slips off his thin, black wool jacket. He has a downtown style that would pair well with the woman who was just here. From his gray shirt that hangs low but is fitted tight across his chest, to the boyish grin and messy dark hair. He's sex on a stick for sure.

"It is wonderful to see you in person, thank you so much for meeting me here," I say as I make my way to the front of the shop, making sure not to spill the hot drink in my hand.

"Finally meeting my maybe new agent," he says with both an asymmetric smile and pride.

"I'm so happy you're thinking of signing with us," I answer sweetly.

"The rain this fall is ridiculous," Jacob states as he runs his hand over his hair and then wipes it off on his worn jeans.

His white Chuck Taylor sneakers squeak on the floor as he takes a step closer to me. His expression is comical. With both hands full, one of chai and the other with the muffin top, I gesture to the table where I already have my laptop set up. "Right over here," I tell him and put both the chai and the pastry to the left side of my computer before turning around to face him.

I have to crane my neck. "You're so much taller in person," I tell him and hold out a hand for a handshake. His right hand engulfs mine and his shake is firm.

The grin on his face grows to a wide smile and his perfect teeth flash back at me.

He's damn good looking and the fact that his face isn't anywhere on his profiles or brand is a mistake. I watch him as I take my seat, keeping the smile where it belongs on my expression.

"You are too good looking for every one of your readers not to see your face. I know this is a meeting to see if you're interested in coming on board and if our goals align, but the way I like to approach things is to treat you like a client from the start so you know what you're getting. There's so much we have to offer at the agency and I'm sure you'll appreciate not wasting time."

"I like to know what I'm getting; let's dive in. What do you want from me, Katerina?" Jacob asks me and for a split second, a thought enters my mind.

It's only a fraction of a second. A glimpse of his mouth on mine, his hands on my body. Pushing me against the wall like Evan did only a few nights ago.

Thankfully, it vanishes before I can show any admission of what I was thinking.

With a deep inhale, I shake off the unwanted thought and I focus on the plan I have laid out for him as I rotate the computer around on the table.

"We're going to start with your strengths. Obviously. your writing is one of them. Let's also work our way into other aspects of marketing and social media that I think you're ignoring. We can come up with a solid plan that you're comfortable with, but more importantly, one that will work to give you momentum before this upcoming release."

The words come out of my mouth smoothly even though my mind's racing.

It's been a while since I've looked at a man and thought the things running through my head. I tell myself it's because I'm looking for comfort. Searching for someone to desire me like Evan does.

So I don't feel trapped and alone.

"Lead the way, Miss Thompson."

I shake my head, ready to correct him, ready to tell him it's *Mrs.* Thompson. Instead I bite my tongue. In fact, I find myself hiding my left hand behind the computer.

It's only because the attention is nice.

A distraction, a sweet voice whispers in the back of my head as I smile at Jacob and hit the right arrow on the keyboard to move to the first point I want to make.

I leave my hand where it's hidden and when he tells me goodbye, again referring to me as "Miss," I still don't correct him.

Chapter 16

Evan

She makes my blood heat,
My breathing tense and ragged.
Love's not a straight line,
It's reckless and it's jagged.
Beyond the lust, beyond desire,
There's something in its wake.
It's jealousy that makes me weak,
It's hate that makes me break.

Brew Madison is my wife's favorite place in this whole damn city. My shoes smack on the wet pavement and rain spits from the sky as I close the door a block down and stride down the sidewalk to the coffee shop.

For years she's come here. She and Jules used to write

together in the corner. Jules was her first client here in New York. It's how she met her now close friend. I huff and my breath turns to steam as I peek in through the glass window.

It used to be a habit of mine to stop here before going home when I landed. Nine times out of ten, she'd be in the same back corner, immersed in a book or a contract. Half the time she was in a meeting.

But then things changed. She stopped going out with too much work piling up as her business grew, and I stopped searching for her when I left the airport. I knew she'd be home, stuck in her office and working no matter what time of day it was.

Work will take as much time as you give it. And Kat gives it all her time and then some.

Today is a different day, though. Given I just told my boss to fuck off knowing he has evidence that could get me locked up, I need to find Kat. I have to see her.

Just before I get to the glass door, I spot my wife. But more importantly, I see who she's with.

Some asshole is with her. I'm sure he's only a client, but as they walk toward the exit, Kat's eyes on her purse as she rummages through it, looking for her keys I'd think, his eyes are all over her body.

The bastard licks his lower lip, and his gaze flickers to Kat's breasts and then to her eyes as she peeks up at him.

She smiles so naively and tucks her hair behind her ear,

but what lights up the anger and the possessiveness running through me, is the blush that rises to her cheeks. My body goes cold and my feet turn to cement standing outside of the shop, watching the two of them unknowingly walk toward me.

She knows he's looking. She knows he likes what he sees. And she's letting him.

The chill that runs through my body fuels something deep inside of me. Something primal and raw. The rain that crashes down on me as the clouds roll in and the sky turns darker by the second does nothing to calm the rage growing inside of me.

I open the door just as the two of them are leaving. My grip on the handle is tight and unforgiving as I wait for them to look up at me.

Kat doesn't stop talking, her sweet voice rattling off something about a signing and who needs to be called to schedule some event.

The dick with a hard-on for my wife sees me first, his eyes widening slightly as he takes in my expression. His first instinct is to angle his body, putting himself between me and Kat. It pisses me off even more and I force my body to stay still, keeping myself from shoving him away from her.

My teeth grind against one another as I stare at his hand, still on her lower back as if he has any right to touch her.

"Evan." Kat looks up at me surprised at first, without a hint of anything other than shock, but instantly her expression changes. "What are you doing? You're getting soaked!" she admonishes me in front of the fucker still standing far too close.

Pride flows through me as she pulls me into the coffee shop, even if she's doing it out of frustration.

She looks from my wet shoulders and the rain dripping down my hair to my forehead and back and then glances outside the shop. She hasn't even acknowledged the man she's with. The demon inside me is at least appeased by that small fact. Her small hands focus on wiping off as much water as she can as she positions me over the large welcome mat at the front of the store.

"Nice to meet you," I say to the man eyeing the two of us. "I'm Kat's husband."

Kat looks up at me and it's obvious she bites her tongue from how her expression scrunches.

"Didn't know she was married," the fucker says and I read him loud and clear. I knew there was a crack in my marriage. But this shit isn't something I'm going to let ruin us. It takes everything in me not to be aggressive toward this shithead.

Kat turns a bright shade of red, but instead of defending us and our relationship, instead of taking my side, she says the worst thing she could to me right now.

"I don't know what we are right now," she states more to me than to him as she looks me in the eyes, daring me to say another word. When I'm quiet, she turns to him.

"I'm sorry for the interruption, Jacob."

"Jake, you can call me Jake," he answers and doesn't even bother to look at me. The awkward tension heats. The thumping of blood rushing in my ears is accompanied with an uncomfortable heat. It was between us. Our problem was only between us. And she made it known to him?

"I'll touch base with you after I get the schedule drawn up, and make sure you get me those summaries as soon as you're able to."

Jake nods his head at Kat and then looks at me to say, "Nice to meet you." He takes his time leaving, glancing over his shoulder more than once, with the rain now coming down in sheets.

"You don't know what we are?" I ask her, feeling the rage wane as the door closes and the sound of the rain is muffled again.

"When you make an ass out of yourself in front of a client, what do you expect me to do?" she hisses.

The rain gets harder and louder as we stand off to the side of the entrance. I take a look around and there are only two other people in the entire place. Both of them women who look like they're on a lunch break, dressed for office jobs. One on each side of the room, both of them on their phones and one with headphones in her ears.

"We can wait out the rain. Get a cup of coffee?" I ask her.

At first Kat looks up at me like I'm crazy. Maybe I am.

"And do what?" she asks. "Play let's-keep-a-secret and

hide-away-for-days?"

I ignore her brutal tone and take a chance, wrapping my arm around her waist.

She jumps back for a second, but only because I'm soaking wet.

I chuckle at her response, deep and rough and it makes her smile. She's quick to hide it, but it's there.

"I know you're mad at me," I tell her softly. "I don't want to make you angry, Kat. I love you, and I'm trying."

The trace of all humor fades and she peeks up at me and whispers, "I wish you wouldn't."

I brush the hair from her face and smile down at her as I tell her, "I'll never stop fighting for you."

At my words, she pushes away from me and says, "Then let's talk until the rain lets up." She looks over her shoulder and out of the window, as if checking to see if our time is already up.

We head to the back corner of the shop, to her spot and her safe place. I can't count the number of times I've sat here with her while she rambled on and told me about her day. Although that was before. It's been too long.

The rest of the seating in the place is all high-top tables and bar-height seats, but in the corner is an L-shaped booth. The same shiny white tabletop, but the seating is for customers who want to spend a while in here and that's what I need with her right now, more time.

She doesn't look at me as she tosses her purse into the booth and then fishes out her wallet.

"You like him?" I question, feeling small pieces of my heart crumble off. Kat's eyes narrow as she huffs out a breath of frustration.

"Knock it off," she answers and I feel torn. I saw the look in her eyes. She's a natural flirt and so am I, but I know she liked the attention more than she should. She felt comfortable with it.

"I don't like him."

"Good to know," she answers me immediately, crossing her arms as she walks toward the counter to order something.

I follow her like a lost fucking puppy. It's quiet between us and the tension is thick as she orders a coffee or whatever the hell it is. The blood is pounding so hard in my ears, I can't hear a damn thing.

"I mean it. He wants you, Kat," I tell her and then nearly flinch from the look in her eyes. "I don't want anyone else's hands on you."

"It was innocent."

"The hell it was," I bite back instantly, keeping my voice low. I don't give her a chance to speak.

"You can't look me in the eyes and tell me you didn't like it." The air between us turns hot instantly.

"He's a client," she says beneath her breath. My eyes dart from her to the man behind the counter. As soon as I look at him, he averts his eyes, pretending like he didn't just hear the venom in Kat's voice.

"Client or not," I say, standing my ground but all it does is wind Kat up more.

"I'm not the one keeping secrets and lying, I'm not the one who's breaking up this marriage," she says much lower, so much so that it sounds like it was hard for her to even get the words out.

"Stop it," I tell her and grip her hip as she tries to walk past me, back to the booth and undoubtedly to get her stuff and leave.

"I'm sorry," I whisper in her ear and hold her closer to me. I splay my hand on her lower back, feeling the tension in her body slowly leave her. Her body is hot next to mine.

I could fight this, but it's not worth it to upset her. I wait, giving her a moment to calm down and forget about that asshole. For now.

I sit back in the seat, watching the steam rise from her cup as she slips the lid off and grabs a packet of sugar from the center of the table.

The packet makes a flapping sound as she shakes it back and forth between her forefinger and thumb to get the sugar down. The motion is forceful and she stares at it as she does it, before finally ripping it open and dumping the sugar into the cup.

"I don't tell you everything." The words slip out as the need to win her back takes over everything else.

She's still for a moment, waiting for more, but not looking

me in the eyes.

"It's not like I do anything that's ... that I want to hide from you. You know what it's like when I go to work."

"I know," Kat says with zero trace of a fight in her voice. "I remember."

"I loved it when you came out with me. You know that, right?"

She finally looks up at me, but only for a moment before she nods her head then slips on the cap to her coffee cup. Her voice is full of remorse as she tells me, "I don't have time for that anymore."

I love that her mind immediately went to the thought of me asking her to come with me. At the beginning of this year, that's all I wanted from her. So we could spend more time together and I could show her off. But the answer was always "no, I can't take time off" so I stopped asking. My heart thumps hard in my chest, remembering how we got into a fight over her not wanting to come with me to Rome a few months back.

"I gave my notice," I tell her and her eyes fly to mine, looking accusing more than anything. "Because you wanted me to." I say the words as if they're the truth and for a moment it feels like they are. But then I remember that's not the reason. I remember what happened. I remember everything in a flood and I have to turn away to breathe in deep and focus on keeping Kat. That's the only thing I care about while everything else collapses around me.

"And because I want to quit too."

"When's your last day?" There's a small bit of hope in her voice, and I watch it shatter as I hesitate to answer.

"I don't know. He ... umm. James." I run my hand down the back of my head and I hate how Kat sees through it all. Her head shakes with disappointment. "It's not finalized."

I nearly forget everything I planned on telling her, but somehow I hold on to it and continue, "I regret a lot of the things I've done this year and maybe for a while now—"

"For a while?" Kat repeats and her eyes reflect the pain that's in her voice.

"I didn't cheat on you, Kat. It's not what you think," I tell her and feel like a liar. "I told you, you're the only one for me."

Before I can say anything else, she shakes her head and that false smile mars her face. "I don't know what you did. But I don't want to know anymore," she says quietly, staring at the cup in her hands before looking back up at me. "We're different people and I think it was only a matter of time before something like this ..." her voice cracks, but she doesn't cry. She simply looks away.

My heartbeat slows. So slow that it's painful.

"Where are you sleeping tonight?" Kat asks me and I have to swallow the spiked lump deep down in my throat before I can answer.

"You still don't want me to come home?"

"It would be easier if you didn't."

"Easier for what?"

"Easier for the breakup, Evan." Her lips part and then she adds, "It's not about love anymore or about what we had. It's about trust and what we've become. I need a fresh start and a life I'm proud of. And I don't think it includes you in it."

"It does," I answer her instantly. "And I want the same."

She stares back at me with an expression that shows how vulnerable she is. How much she wants to believe what I'm telling her.

I take her hand in mine and tell her, "I'll do whatever you want, so long as when it's all said and done I get to keep you."

I stare in her eyes knowing I've never said anything more truthful, but something deep down inside tells me that's not how this story will end.

"It's too little, too late, Evan. I'm sorry."

Chapter 17

Kat

The bed groans and dips as I turn back onto my right shoulder, pushing the pillow between my knees and trying to force myself to sleep. My mind won't stop playing back every minute of the coffee shop. Every little moment. Even sleeping pills aren't working.

I've been alone all my life. Until Evan. When he first started sleeping over, it was hard to fall asleep. Unless he fucked me to the point of exhaustion, which was often.

You'd think it'd be easy going back to being alone. I was a pro at it for years and worse yet, I was proud of it. The train goes by and the sound cuts through the white noise of the city. The windows are closed, but I still hear it. I can even feel the rumble and vibrations as I try to lie still on the bed. And that's when I get a hint of Evan's scent. When I'm alone, missing him, I sleep on his side of the bed. It's easiest the first night he's gone. It smells just like him. Each day it gets a little harder and working late nights gets more appealing. But even the masculine scent that drifts toward me as I inch my head closer to his pillow isn't enough to comfort me. Why would it? I'm losing him and everything we had.

I toss the heavy comforter off my body and sit up, wiping the sleep from my eyes and dangling my feet over the side of the bed. It's nearly 1:00 a.m. and pitch black in the room. I should be sleeping, considering the fatigue plaguing my body and all too conscious it should come easy.

My fingers run through my long hair, separating it and braiding it loosely before I take a sip of water from the glass on the nightstand. If I get up and start working, I know I won't sleep at all tonight. The very thought makes my heart thump harder. Work is killing me, lack of sleep is destroying me. But both are because I'm completely and utterly alone.

Just breathe. I let my head fall back and slowly creep back under the covers. All I need to do is breathe.

But that hope is short lived as I hear Evan climb the stairs. I had one condition to him coming home, and that was leaving me the bedroom. Even if it hurts me, I'd rather feel pain in his absence than a fraction of that pain in his presence.

I close my eyes as I hear the door open. For a moment I

think I should pretend to be asleep, but I don't want any more lies in our relationship. Whatever our relationship even is now.

"I thought you were going to sleep on the sofa?" I ask him and then hold my breath. I should want him to leave. That's what a sane woman who's getting a divorce should want. But there isn't an ounce of me that wants to see him walk out that door.

"I was going to," Evan answers and then slips his shirt off over his head. He keeps his eyes on me, daring me to say something, but my eyes focus on his broad chest.

In six years his body has changed, as has mine. But he's still lean and muscular. My body heats and my thighs clench, but I play it off, turning my back to him to lie on my left shoulder.

"Is this all right?" he asks me, his voice carrying through the dark night and cutting me down to my deepest insecurity. It's not all right and nothing about this situation is, but those aren't the words that come out of my mouth.

My eyes squeeze shut tight and I give in to what I want, slowly moving my body toward his. Wouldn't it be a lie to deny it?

"I'm afraid I'll like it too much if you stay," I finally answer with my eyes closed as the bed dips. I stay perfectly still as I lay out the bare truth. "I'm afraid I'll forgive you and I'll forget why we shouldn't be together." All the words pour out from deep down in my soul, leaving my lips in a rush.

A rough sound comes from deep in his throat as the

comforter pulls just slightly. "You don't know what you want, Kat," Evan tells me although the confidence is missing. "You want me to leave because you're afraid. You won't fight for me to stay because you know I will regardless of what you say, isn't that right?"

My brow furrows as I take in his assessment. He scoots closer to me, making the bed shift beneath my still body. When I turn to meet him, still under the covers, his dark gaze stares at me as if I'm his prey and that's just how I feel. "No. I want you to leave because we're leading different lives." I have to second-guess my words.

"Then let's get back on track. Let's start over," he whispers and then leans closer to me. As if testing my boundaries, he rests his hand on the pillow above my head. I don't push him away, but I don't move toward him either.

I'm fucked no matter what I do.

I'm empty and hollow. All the sadness and regret has been shed from me, leaving nothing behind but faint memories of what we had and the hint of all the hopes and dreams I had so long ago to make my heart flutter. As I close my eyes and swallow the lump in my throat, Evan lies next to me, gently resting his hand on my hip. He's silent but I can hear his steady breath and smell a hint of his scent. I inhale deeper. God, what that scent does to me. My head dips further into the pillow as I readjust under the covers and when I do, Evan lifts his hand slightly. Waiting to see which way I'll turn.

And I turn toward him.

"You make me a foolish woman," I tell him as my eyes slowly open. His hazel eyes are so clear at this angle. Maybe it's the moon creeping in from the slit between the curtains.

He smirks at me, although there's a sadness in his smile as he brushes my hair from my face.

"Tell me you'll stay with me."

"Tell me why I should," I reply instantly and the soft look of longing in his eyes fades away as the soothing motion of his thumb rubbing along my temple falters. My eyes drop to his chest and my heart plummets to the pit of my stomach. "You said you didn't cheat," I tell him, but mostly I make a promise to myself. "So I believe you."

"Thank you," he says so softly beneath his breath I hardly hear him. His shoulders sag slightly and it makes the bed creak with relief.

I want to say more. I want to make some sort of demand or ultimatum ... or ask why he was there in that hotel lobby in the middle of the night. Why he lied to the world. Why he's lying to me. But instead I curl into him.

"Don't leave me," he says, giving me the request and wraps his arms around me, pulling me closer to him. Closer to his scent, his warmth, to the man I've been desperate to be with for so damn long. His heat wraps around me in the most comforting of ways.

"I won't promise you that," I answer with honesty with

my eyes open, staring at a small scar on his left shoulder. I lift my hand up and let my fingers play along the silvery indent of it. "You're right that I don't know what I want. So we'll just have to find out."

He's quiet for a long time. And part of my heart, a very large part of it, aches. It's a horrible feeling and it makes my eyes sting. But I won't mourn what I'm not even sure I've lost. It's just the threat of ending something I've valued so dearly and for so long that hurts.

My shoulders shake slightly as I take in a shuddering breath, and that's when he cups my chin and forces me to look at him.

"You know I love you," he says with a ragged breath. "More than anything, anything in the world."

I sniffle and try to ignore how the pain grows. "I do," I tell him and then try to hide my face, but his grip on my chin is too strong and I can only close my eyes, feeling the smallest bit of tears threaten to spill over and soak into my lashes.

"Don't cry, Kat," Evan whispers as he rests his forehead against mine. "I love you, and that's all that matters." For some reason it seems so obvious to me in this moment that those words were more for him than they were for me. My eyes open to find his still closed. To see the pain there. To see how desperate he is.

That's what I can blame it on. And it's my undoing.

It always has been. He needs me, and I crave it.

"Kiss me—" Before the command leaves my lips, his are on mine. Devouring me and taking every little piece I'm willing to give. I crumble underneath him. My hands fly to his hair as he deepens the kiss. The air turns hotter as my skin heats and our breathing quickens.

"Kat." He barely breaks away from me to whisper my name and then presses his lips harder against mine as he grabs my hips and pulls me toward him.

My gasp is muted as his tongue dives into my mouth. My back arches and my breasts push against his hard chest as he climbs on top of me.

Every second I'm acutely aware that I'm falling backward. It pains my heart as I pull away from him, digging my head into the pillow to feel the cool air. But I can't stop this. I never could. He nips along my neck and my body clenches with need as my legs wrap around his waist.

My heels dig into his ass while I close my eyes tight and let my body do what it wants. It's only ever wanted him and I won't deny my own needs.

Not when he worships me like this, kissing his way down my body as he strips the clothes from me. The only sound is our breathing as I cautiously open my eyes to watch.

His fingertips brush against my skin as he takes off the last piece and stares at my glistening sex.

"You're wet for me." He says the words out loud, although I don't think he meant for me to hear. Another time, I'd blush. But there's no shame or embarrassment right now. It's desperation.

He parts from his clothes faster than I can steady my breath. The moonlight casts shadows on his chiseled chest and every sensitive bit of me is on fire and singing with need. My eyes are drawn to his hands as he strokes his length. When he does it again, I can't help how my lips part with desire and my legs spread wider. My body's ready, willing and aching for him to take me.

"I'm the only one who can satisfy you like this, Kat." My gaze shifts to Evan and he captures it with an intensity that pins me down. "Don't ever forget that."

I can't respond, I don't have time. In one swift motion he's buried to the hilt inside of me. Stretching my walls and sending a spike of heat, desire and a bit of pain through me. Every nerve ending screams to life as a strangled moan tears through me.

It's nothing but pleasure as he stills deep inside of me. Waiting for me to adjust to his girth. He takes his time kissing his way up my collarbone to my lips.

The touches are softer now. Small pecks and nips until I open my eyes and he brings them to a halt.

"I love you," he whispers. My legs wrap around his waist and my fingers dig into his strong shoulders as he moves slowly at first. Burying his head into my neck before I can tell him the same.

He rocks his hips, his rough pubic hair rubbing against my clit with each small movement and bringing me higher and higher. My release feels so close but so far away just the same.

I can only make small whimpers as he speeds up, knowing he's going to send me crashing in the end. All the while he rides through my orgasm, fueled by my cries of pleasure. I cling to him for dear life as my body seems paralyzed and he continues to take from me. Pounding into me, harder and harder. Pistoning his hips until the headboard slams against the wall rhythmically in time with his relentless thrusts. He has his way with me, and then he holds me. I would do it all again just for this moment in time. Just to be held by him, as if he'll never let me go.

Chapter 18

Evan

It's been a long damn time since I've made breakfast for Kat. It's probably been a year or more since we've woken up together, that's how fucked our schedules have become.

Her bare feet pad down the stairs as I set the last plate on the table. It's brimming with fresh diced pineapple and strawberries. Bacon's still the prominent scent, though. Bacon and eggs for breakfast. Plus a platter of hotcakes with fruit in the center and of course, her coffee.

I grab her mug from her spot on the table. It's still burning hot but I make sure to put it handle out as I turn around to face her. Maybe I'm pussywhipped. Maybe I'm sucking up. Either way, I don't give a fuck.

The sight of her messy halo of hair and wide eyes with a bit of mascara still lingering from yesterday makes my heart pump hard in my chest. She's gorgeous even when she's a mess. She's got nothing on but a baggy Henley of mine and it makes her seem even more petite than she already is. My Kat's never been an early riser. Only when she has to, or apparently when the smell of breakfast is in the air.

"You have good timing," I tell her as she hesitantly grabs the coffee. I can see her shoulders sag just a bit and her eyes close as she takes in the smell, though. It gives me a sense of pride. Even if it's just for the moment.

"Good morning," she says with a soft smile, but it's barely hiding her true feelings. I force a smile back and pull out her chair.

"I don't know the last time I had an actual breakfast," she says as she takes the seat and then looks up at me. "Thank you." It's genuine, but with her shoulders hunched and that sad look in her eyes, I don't give her a response.

I wish I could hold on to last night forever. But the sun had to rise, and I need to come clean to her. She deserves that much.

The chair legs scratch on the wooden floor as I pull out my seat. I grimace slightly and then clear my throat as I sit down, noticing how Kat doesn't seem to care. She's not nearly awake enough; sleep still dominates her expression.

With both hands cradling her mug, she leans back in her

seat and gives me a small smile but doesn't reach for any food. She doesn't say anything either. All she does is wait. I wish I had something better to offer her than what's going to come out of my mouth.

"I want a fresh start ... and the marriage we were supposed to have," I say as I push a fork through the pancake on my plate, but I don't eat it. I'm already sick to my stomach.

A heavy breath leaves me and I rub my forehead to get out some of the tension. I can't tell her everything, but I can give her something that has killed me for years; a truth I wish didn't exist.

My skin's hot and my throat's dry. It's been years, and I never intended on telling Kat. I didn't want her to know and it was before things changed for me. Before my mother told me she was dying. Before Kat came to me and showed me she was the person I needed in my life forever. It happened before I realized she was mine and I was never going to let her go.

"You okay?" Kat asks and there's genuine pain in her voice. Sadness and concern I wish weren't there. She's too good for me. I've made so many mistakes and this is going to crush her and hurt her more than it should. It meant nothing to me back then, but it'll mean everything to her right now. And I hate it.

"There's something I have to tell you." As I say the words I look Kat in the eyes, and her expression changes. The corners of her lips turn down and a deep crease settles between her brows. She has this way of hiding her emotions, but it doesn't last long. She offers me a hard stare with her lips pressed into a thin line. She gives it to me all the time, but I know the second I give her silence, Kat's mouth will open and every emotion she's feeling will show. She can't hide it from me.

"When you asked me about Samantha, if I'd slept with her ..." I have to break off from my thought and pause to take in another breath.

The clink of Kat's fork hitting the plate makes my chest feel tight. She lets out a small sound, almost like a sigh but weighted down with a bitter hopelessness.

"I told you the truth, that I haven't been with anyone since we got married," I say and watch her eyes, her expression, everything about her, but she doesn't look back at me. Her shoulders rise like she's holding her breath and waiting for a bomb to go off.

"It was years ago, Kat. Before I knew how much you meant to me." The words come up my throat as if they're scratching and clawing to stay buried down deep inside of me.

Her expression crumples the second I hint at the affair. If you can even call it that. "I felt like I was lying to you. Every. Single. Time." I bang my fist on the table and the plates rattle with each word and make Kat jump, but I can't help it. "I felt like a bastard when I looked you in the eyes and said nothing happened, because you should have already known."

"When?" Kat asks me.

"I swear that night in the papers was about something else. Something that has nothing to do with that woman or sleeping with her. It was—"

"When?" She screams out the question as her eyes gloss over. She doesn't stop staring at me, but the emotion I expect to see isn't there. It's only anger, a furious rage that stares back at me. "When did you sleep with her?"

"The night I got the call from my mother." I swallow thickly and add, "I was with her."

"The night she told you?" she asks me with a morbid tone and I nod, feeling that acidic churning in my stomach as my clammy hands clench. "You were at the company party?" she asks instantly, although it's more of her recalling that night than an actual question.

"You were supposed to take me out that night afterward," Kat says and each word sounds sadder and sadder as she looks away from me. "You were fucking her while at work."

"It was a one-time thing. A mistake. I didn't know who she was and things were getting serious with us, Kat. You don't understand. It wasn't how it seems." I stumble over my words. Leaning closer to her and reaching for her, she abruptly pushes away from the table, slamming her palms against it and scooting the chair back.

My hands fly into the air, keeping them up. As if I'm not a threat. Trying to keep her here with me to give me a chance to explain.

"Look, we were getting serious and I needed … I don't know how to explain it."

"You didn't want to be with me anymore so you went and slept with the first girl to bat her eyelashes at you?" she asks although it's less of a question and more an accusation, a bitter one at that.

I can't explain how pathetic I feel as she looks at me like I'm the devil. It was a game back then. I wish I could change it. If I'd known what Kat would mean to me, I'd have put a ring on her finger the moment I laid eyes on her. I never would have done anything to risk what we had. *Lies. So many lies*, a voice in the back of my mind whispers. If that was the truth, I wouldn't have needed to call Samantha with my eyes on a lifeless body in the corporate hotel room. If she knew everything, she'd hate me.

"I messed up and I made a lot of mistakes," I say and lean toward her, but she's not having it.

"How many women have you fucked since I've been with you?" Her voice is hard and full of nothing but bitterness.

"Just her, just Samantha and just that once. Please, Kat." My voice begs her for mercy as I lean forward but she's quick to stand up, nearly toppling the chair over just so she can get away from me.

Regret consumes me. I wish I hadn't told her. Fuck. I don't know what to wish for anymore.

I swallow thickly and try to remember everything else I

was going to say and the point of bringing up the past. "It's why I feel so guilty about these allegations and why I didn't say anything to the press. I needed them to think it'd happened and it kind of did, just years ago."

"Why were you in the hotel lobby with her at three in the morning?" she asks me—for the dozenth time—as she crosses her arms over her chest, bunching the shirt and finally letting her gaze trap mine.

I have to swallow the hard lump in my dry throat before I can answer her. "I needed an alibi."

"Are you fucking serious, Evan?" she says, spitting out her words as she looks at me with more disgust than I've ever seen on her face.

"I'm sorry. It was an accident."

"It's always an accident. Always a mistake. Why do you do this? Why do you put yourself in these situations?" She screams at me with a rage I know she's had pent up inside of her for a while now. I'm too old to be this stupid. I never should have continued working for James once her career took off. But the money and the lifestyle were so addictive. It was a high I couldn't refuse.

"I told you, I quit. I'm not going to put myself in—" As I shake my head, trying to get out the words, I can't remember a damn thing I'd planned on saying.

"It's too little, too late, Evan," Kat says, cutting me off before leaving me alone in the room, whipping around and not bothering to say another word. I stare at her back as she storms up the stairs.

I've never felt this way before in my life. Like I've hurt the one person in the world who would never hurt me. Like I betrayed her. Like I'm not worth a damn thing.

And there's no way to make that right.

I don't know how to make any of this right.

Chapter 19

Kat

I knew the truth,
I didn't want to believe.
But deep in my gut,
The agony did seethe. Call me a fool,
Say what you will.
But I can't help it,
I love him still.

I can't stop thinking about how Evan fucked her. Samantha is … the opposite of me. Everything about her is exactly the opposite. Disgust doesn't begin to cover it. All I can imagine is how that night would have played out had his mother not called him. If tragedy hadn't stepped in to intervene. He fucked her, and then what? Was he going to bail on our date or was he still planning on seeing me?

I should be focused on the fact that he told me he needed an alibi. The fact that only weeks ago he was doing shit he knows is wrong and could send him to jail. But that's the man he's always been. I knew better than to turn a blind eye, but that's exactly what I've been doing, isn't it?

It's an odd feeling, like waking up from a long and deep sleep or having a blindfold taken off after wearing it for days. Has it always been this way?

I knew what kind of life he was leading and the risks that came with it. I didn't do a damn thing about it. I should be ashamed, mortified.

And yet all I can think about is him fucking her.

Not to mention how many times I've seen that woman at events and socialized with her. Not once did she make it seem like anything had happened between them. She comes off sweet and innocent. She's slim like me, but taller and she prefers soft, muted colors. Samantha always has perfectly manicured, pale pink nails. She pretties herself up like a little doll, prim and proper. I never would have expected it. I remember how genuinely happy for me she seemed when she gushed over my engagement ring.

That fucking bitch.

The door to my office opens behind me, the telltale creak forcing my eyes to shoot open. They narrow as I see his reflection on the black computer screen. I don't even know if the damn thing is on anymore or how long I've been sitting here. All I've done is stare at a worn spot on my desk and think about how he fucked her, even knowing he was going to see me only hours later.

What would have happened if his mother hadn't chosen that moment to tell him to come home and that she wasn't well? Maybe that would have been the night he chose to break it off with me. After all, every day with him was like ticking off a checkbox. I knew it wasn't going to last. I was waiting for it to end.

Marie screwed me over by telling him.

"Kat." Evan calls my name from behind me. Hearing his voice causes a shudder to run down my spine. It's a slow one that sends a chill over my body.

"I'm going to do everything I can to prove to you how much I love you."

"Do I even know you?" Even as I whip around and sneer at him a sick voice in the back of my head answers me. *Yes. Yes, you knew what you were doing. You knew the man you married.*

"You're the only one who does," he answers, looking me in the eyes as his broad shoulders fill the doorframe to my office. "You know I love you."

I scoff at him, choosing to ignore the truth and how much I blame myself.

Right now, it's all on him. I didn't cheat on him. I didn't continue to live a lifestyle that was obviously going to tear us apart.

He did. And fuck him for that.

"I hate you right now." The words slip out in a breath and he visibly flinches.

"You're angry, and you have every right to be."

"Angry doesn't cut it!" I scream, my throat feeling raw as the salty tears burn my eyes. "I loved you. I would have done anything for you!" I grit out the words through my clenched teeth and try to grip the chair as I stand on shaky legs.

"I loved you so much. And this is how you treat our marriage. With lies and secrets and all this shit I don't even know about."

"I'm sorry I kept that from you, but that was it." He says *that was it* as if it's easily accepted. As if he's never told a lie or done anything else that would ruin us.

"Liar! How many laws have you broken at work?" I let the words tumble from my mouth, all the rage coursing through my blood. "But you kept at it. You were never going to stop until something made you. You didn't care about me or what it did to us!

"What kind of marriage is that!" As the words tear from my throat and Evan stares back at me a guilty man, the reality hits me like a bullet to the chest.

I was blinded by my lust for him. Maybe even my love. Either way, I've been denying the reality.

"I want more than this. I deserve better."

"I love you," he says like that's the answer to all of this. Like it will save us.

"You keep saying that, but I don't think you know what it means." *Or maybe love just simply isn't enough anymore.*

"What really gets me," I start to say then take in a long, ragged breath, finally taking a step toward him but immediately stop when he does the same.

Standing across from him in the small office I look him in the eyes and get what I've been thinking about out of me. "You saw her all the time. You were with her at every function." My voice lowers as I add, "Even *I* was with her so many times. And you didn't bother to tell me."

"What happened was a mistake for her too."

"Don't talk to me like she didn't know what she was doing. She was married and she knew we were together. How could you? How could you stand to be around her?"

"I was working. If you'll recall, you were broke and we needed money. What was I supposed to do? Quit?"

"Does your boss know?" His expression turns to stone, although he looks more pissed off than anything else. "Does James know?" I ask him again.

"I don't know."

It's silent as I breathe out a huff of disgust.

"I'm sorry. I fucked up but it was years ago."

"It wasn't just years ago. Every day you went back was a mistake. Every day you kept it from me was a mistake!"

"What part of it being my job don't you get?" he asks me in a low voice full of anger as he takes another step forward.

"You could have gotten another job." All I can see is red. The words come out automatically, but my mind is racing. My breathing is heavy.

"Who would hire me?" he asks with sincerity. "You were just starting out and needed every penny I could earn."

"Don't act like you did this for me!" I spit at him with anger. My fist pounds against my chest. "Don't you dare blame this on me!"

Tears prick my eyes as he stares at me without saying a word.

Shame and guilt heat my body. Both of us are raging with emotion. Both of us want to tear the other person apart. That realization is all I can take. Tears spill over and I have to turn away from him. With my back to him, he tries to touch me and I rip my arm away from him. I shake my head and firm my resolve.

"Please leave me alone. I'm begging you, Evan. If you love me, please get away from me."

Chapter 20

Evan

> The truth I cannot change,
> I'm a sinner and I confess.
> But I refuse to let her go,
> She's my love and nothing less.

I love you, Kat, and I'm sorry.

I text her again, the cellphone screen lighting up the dark bedroom in Pops's house, my old bedroom. The glossy posters reflect the light that scatters into the room in stripes from the blinds on the window. The sound of the traffic is louder here and everything about it reminds me of the life I used to lead. The one before Kat. The one I'm so damn ashamed of now.

I'll never forget the look of disappointment on his face when I showed up a few hours ago with a duffle bag. It's like even he lost hope in me making it right with Kat.

It's crushing to leave her. But it's different this time. I get exactly why she needs space. This is why I never told her. She needed something to hold on to, though, she needed a solid reason to be pissed at me, so we could get through it and move on.

Still, I didn't expect it to go down like it did. I'm worthless and it's never been more apparent to me that my life is meaningless without Kat in it.

I swallow thickly as I lean back on the bed and fall against the pillow. I've never felt so alone. I wish I could take it all back.

My eyes close as I feel my heart slow and my blood turn cold. Being here like this makes me remember one of the last conversations I had with my mother.

She'd seen me with Kat while we were out one night. Just a coincidence, but she acted like it was more than it was.

Kat was a fling and a good time. She was someone I wanted more and more of and I made damn sure to monopolize her time until I had my fill, but of course that time would never come. I just didn't know it back then or I liked to pretend I didn't anyway.

"She seems sweet," my mother told me when I came home for Sunday dinner. Looking back at that night now, I realize how much slower she was to set the table. How everything was a little off, but to me, Sunday dinner was just an obligation I had to my mother before I would be leaving to go out and have a good time.

"You didn't really talk to her," I said and laughed at my mom, shaking my head and taking a drink from whatever was in my cup. I leaned back and looked at my father, waiting for him to agree with me. When he didn't, I added, "Plus she's the only girl you've seen me with."

"That's true," Ma replied and shrugged. "I like the way you two look together," she stated matter-of-factly and then looked me in the eyes as she smiled. "Is it too much to ask that you pretend to value your mother's opinion?"

I let out a small laugh and shook my head. "I'm glad you approve," I told her. More just to make her happy than anything else, but it only opened the door for Ma to invite her over for the next family dinner. I had already started coming up with reasons to end it that night.

It was too much. I was young and in my prime and working a job that would keep my appetite well-fed.

I was ready to end it too the next night; it was too serious, too soon. But her smile and the way she laughed at me when I pulled up wearing an old rugby shirt caught me off guard in a way I found completely endearing. She thought it was the oddest thing and I'll never forget the way her soft voice hummed with laughter and it carried into the night. Who was I to take that away? I knew she'd end it with me anyway. I didn't know it would be after marriage and six years later.

If I could go back to that night, I would change it all and

I'd make sure I told Ma she was right.

"I'm heading to bed." My father's voice catches me by surprise and my body jolts from the memory. I pretend to rub the sleep from my burning eyes and clear my throat to tell my father good night. It's tight with emotion and it takes me a second to sit up in bed.

"You look like hell," Pops says.

Nodding in agreement, I take a moment to set my feet on the floor. My head is still hung low and my shoulders are sagging as I rest my elbows on my knees.

"How did you keep Ma out of it? All the stupid shit you did?" I ask him. I know he led a wild life. He's got the stories and the scars to prove it. I came by my lifestyle honestly.

I lift my head and look him in the eyes, forcing a small smile to my face. "I need to know what to do. I need advice."

"You can't. It's gotta stop." He shrugs his shoulders, the faint light from the hallway casting a long shadow of him into the room, ending at my feet. "That's the advice I can give you. Don't keep a thing from her. You should already know that."

I swallow, or try to, as a ball of spikes grows in my throat. "What if you can't stop? What if I can't quit this job and this life?" The image of Tony dead on the floor remains firm in my sight. Even as I blink it away and look up at my father, I can still see him. Dead from an overdose and staring back at me with glassy, lifeless eyes as if it was my fault.

I brought him to that room. The one reserved for partying

in our company.

I gave him the coke, but I didn't know it was laced. And then I left him there to get whiskey and cigarettes.

I brought him to his death.

I can never tell her that. I can barely admit it to myself.

"Did you ever mess up so bad, you thought you could never make it right?" I ask even though his answer doesn't matter. I guess I just don't want to feel so alone.

"We all do; you just find a way. I'm sorry, but it's the best I've got."

"Find a way ..." I say the words softly, barely moving my lips as I look at the edge of the comforter, wishing it were that easy.

"I don't know what to tell you, Evan. I did everything for your mom, and I'd do it all again. Maybe that's where you went wrong?"

"What's that?" I'm quick to ask him, my gaze focused on Pops and whatever it is he has to say. I'm desperate for an answer to all this shit. I need to take it all back.

"You weren't thinking about her."

His words sink in slow, but deep.

I shake my head and agree, "No, I wasn't."

"The best thing you ever did was marry that girl." I nod my head, feeling a jagged pain move through my body. "Worse thing you ever did was leave her side."

He doesn't know how true his words are.

Chapter 21

Kat

> You left a space beside me,
> You left me all alone.
> You left a space beside me,
> I thought my heart would turn to stone.
> You left a space beside me,
> Desire creeps in the night.
> You left a space beside me,
> Lust fills the emptiness up just right.

The evening skyline is gorgeous. The colors of autumn dance along the buildings and the beautiful hues of orange and soft reds travel up to the bright full moon.

It's early for the moon to be out, but as I walk away from the townhouse, down the stone steps as the heavy walnut door shuts behind me, I can't help but admire it. There's beauty in nature and having the small bit of it above the city is something I've taken for granted for so long.

With each step, my boots click on the concrete, until my body stumbles forward and I nearly fall down the last two stairs.

"Shoot!" I cry out as I frantically reach for the iron rail and just barely get a grip tight enough to keep me upright. My purse is flung down to the crook of my arm, spilling odds and ends, including my phone, onto the busy street.

I curse beneath my breath as my cheeks heat with embarrassment and I keep my head down. Most people walk around me, and I'm fine with that. Better than fine. I'm happy that they're just ignoring me and my clumsiness.

I crouch down low to grab the fallen items, ignoring the bystanders as they steer clear of me but as I stand up, I realize someone didn't miss my fall and their eyes haven't left me.

"You okay?" Jacob asks as he comes toward me, nearly out of breath. His cheeks are slightly red, the chill of the air getting to him. His hand is cold on my shoulder as he helps me stand upright. His thick black wool jacket brushes against mine and the heavy scent of pine, a masculine fragrance I love, fills my lungs.

"I saw you from across the street," he tells me as I blink away my surprise. Not only from his presence, but from my reaction.

I brush the hair from my face and give him a grateful smile as the crowd continues to walk around us. This city doesn't stop for anything or anyone. Jacob walks with me to move out of the way and stand on the stairs to my townhome.

"Just a clumsy moment," I say in a breathy voice and reluctantly laugh at myself as I steady the bag back onto my shoulder. This is so embarrassing.

Jacob shrugs and slips his hands into his pockets as he says, "I expected worse." As he speaks, his perfect teeth show, and I can't help but eye his lush lips. "Honestly, that was a nice save."

A warmth flows through me.

"Well thanks," I say, shifting my weight and shaking my head. "What are you doing here?"

"I'm checking out a townhouse down the street. Moving to the city was definitely the right move for me."

"And have you thought of the contract at all?" I ask him and then bite the inside of my cheek. "I don't mean to be forward. I'm just excited to work together."

I don't miss how his eyes stray slightly to my breasts when I breathe in deep. He turns away, toward the street to try to play it off and licks his lower lip. Maybe it was a subconscious thing on my part. I almost feel the need to apologize.

"I'm thinking I should get to signing it. I just was hoping maybe we could meet up to go over a few minor details?" he asks as he brings his attention back to me.

I smile and nod my head, my hair falling back in front of my shoulders. "I'd be happy to," I answer a little too eagerly. His eyes flash with something they shouldn't, but I ignore it.

"Well, I should get going," I say and the words rush out of my mouth.

"Me too," Jacob says and looks back across the street. "My realtor is over there somewhere waiting on the steps to let me in to 'my dream home,'" he says, mimicking what must be his realtor's nasally voice, and then he gives me another view of his gorgeous smile.

"If you ever need anything, I'm always home or a call away," I offer and then bite the inside of my cheek. *What the hell was that?*

"Sounds good. Be safe," he says comically and then takes a few steps forward. "I'll text you," he says over his shoulder and I simply nod. Not able to speak, just standing there, gripping my purse strap with both hands and wondering why he gets to me so much.

I won't deny that he does.

That's not the part that bothers me.

It's why. Is it him? The timing?

What is it about Jacob that makes me want him, when I haven't lusted for a man other than my husband in years?

Chapter 22

Evan

"Have you tried roses?"

My gaze moves from the cell phone in my hand to my father. With his arm braced against the wall, he taps his knuckles against the cream wall.

"I'm not sure roses are going to help," I reply and give him a weak smile.

"You'd be surprised. Flowers are a girl's best friend."

A small but genuine smile graces my lips as I toss the phone onto the end table. "It's diamonds, Pops. The saying is diamonds are a girl's best friend."

"Then get her diamonds," he replies with a stern look before making his way to the worn, caramel-colored leather recliner in the corner of the living room. There's a game on the TV. I'm not sure who's playing since the volume is so low I can barely hear it.

"She still hasn't messaged you back?" he asks.

"Nothing yet," I answer lowly, not bothering to hide my disappointment, and then look back at the phone, wishing it would go off.

"You going back home to talk? Or what's the plan?"

"I don't know," I tell him. "I know she wants space; I just don't know if it's what's best."

From my periphery, I watch him nod and then he says, "It's hard to know. Especially when she's not talking to you."

"I wouldn't talk to me either," I say, mostly out of the need to defend her. "I'd have kicked me out too."

"It was a long time ago," my father says, but there's hardly any conviction in his voice.

It's quiet for longer than I'd like. Both of us not knowing where to go in the conversation.

"I remember when you moved in with her," Pops finally says and breaks the silence.

"It feels like forever ago. I hardly even remember what it was like before her."

"Feels like it just happened to me. All the boxes and her wanting to paint first and then wanting everything in a specific order. She sure has a certain way of going about things."

I lean my head back, staring at the ceiling fan as I say, "Yeah she does" with a hint of a smile on my lips. "She's particular."

"That's one word for it," Pops says back with a small laugh, the kind where I can feel his smile in the laugh, not missing a beat.

"You love her, though. Particular and all," I remind him.

He nods his head. "I love her for it too." He clears his throat and says, "I never told you this, but I felt like I'd lost your mother and then lost you."

"Pops, no—" I try to stop that shit, but he's already moved on before I can get a thought out.

"It was a short-lived feeling. Kat came over more than you did after the move, if you remember."

"She's the one who wanted the family dinners. I remember her pushing for that. Probably wouldn't have happened if it wasn't for her. I think she was just trying to make things right."

"I know she was. She's a lot like your mother in that regard. You did good picking her."

I can't respond to my father. He's never talked to me about Kat really. Now of all times, it's just making the pain that much worse.

"You remember that heavy-ass dresser?" Pops asks me and it makes me huff a laugh as I nod. More than anything I'm thankful for the change in topic.

"She had to have it," I say absently. "It was her mother's."

"Oh, I know. I remember her telling me a dozen times."

"She kept talking about the movers." I shake my

head. "We didn't need any movers."

"Sure, sure. I remember that squabble."

"Squabble," I repeat and run my hand over my hair. "She knew I could handle it."

Pops laughs at the thought. A deep laugh, and then he leans back in his chair.

"You guys can handle that, then you guys can handle anything."

"It feels different, Pops." I swallow and fight back the swell of emotion. "This isn't just a fight."

"How would you know? You haven't even really had a fight, have you?"

I stare at him blankly, knowing me and Kat haven't ever gone at it before, not really. A little bickering here or there, but this isn't some argument over dishes. This is worse than he can imagine, and I'm ashamed to speak that truth.

"Just get her something shiny. Spoil the woman," he says, throwing his hand up.

I let a trace of a smile linger on my lips as I picture handing Kat a bouquet of roses. I'd pick the dark red ones, but make sure there's some baby's breath in the package too. One of the large bouquets. The ones that make you lean in and smell them. Too good to resist. That's the kind I'd get her.

I can see her soft smile as she peeks up at me, holding it in both her hands.

A warmth settles through me. I wish it were that easy. I'd

buy every flower I could if that were the case.

"Whatever you do," Pops says, distracting me from the vision of Kat forgiving me, "just don't give up."

"I won't," I tell him and I damn well mean it.

Chapter 23

Kat

My fingers relentlessly tap on my phone and my gaze drifts to the door. He's coming. Soon.

Evan needs to get his things and get out. Mistake after mistake after mistake. That's what this relationship has been. There's undeniable love between us. I won't argue with that. But some people aren't meant to be together and at this point in my life, I should be concerned with having children and not the possibility of having to bail my husband out of jail.

There's a bit of anger that's carried me through the last two days. It's what I focus on. It's what gives me the strength to tell him I don't want to be with him anymore. To tell him it doesn't matter when he says he loves me.

I know it matters, and I'd be a liar if I didn't admit that I'll always want him and have love for him. I'll always want to feel loved like I did when we first got together.

But there's only one way for the story of the two of us to end and that's with him packing his things and getting out. Loving each other simply isn't enough when we're so far apart in other ways.

As if he heard my thought, the front doorknob jiggles and the sound of keys clinking creeps into the room.

Fate hates me. No, that's not strong enough of a word. It must *loathe* me because the sight of my husband standing in our doorway shatters my heart.

I attempt to keep my expression cold, but my body goes numb and the same coldness that swept over my body only weeks ago when I felt my marriage falling apart drifts over my skin now. His eyes are bloodshot. He can't force a look of anything but agony as he turns his gaze from me and walks slowly into the room, closing the door behind him. The shock to my system is crippling and I can't look him in the eyes. He doesn't try to hide the desperation. His disheveled hair and all-around rough appearance make my body itch to touch him. To comfort him. To make the obvious pain go away.

I think that's why I'll never be able to deny that I love him. The image of him in pain destroys me to my core. My soul hurts for his, and I want nothing more than to take his misery away.

I need to love myself more than I could ever love him. I'm

trying to. My God, am I trying.

He nods his head as he tosses his keys down on the coffee table and stands awkwardly in front of me.

I have to swallow the tightness in my throat and ignore the heat flowing through my body begging me to give in. "Hi." I'm the first to say anything at all and break the uneasy tension in the living room.

"How are you?" he asks and it feels so odd. Like we're just old friends or acquaintances.

"Not the best," I answer him. I try to find that anger, I remember everything as my eyes shift to the entrance to the dining room, but there's not an ounce of anger that will come to my rescue.

"I miss you," he says as the last word spills from my lips.

"I miss you too," I admit, my voice cracking and I lick my lips.

"Things have gotten rough, but I never stopped loving you. You're the only thing that matters."

"What you say is everything I want to hear, Evan. But it's what you've done that makes it impossible for me to stay with you."

His boots smack on the hardwood floor as he makes his way to me. And I don't move. I don't object. I even lean into him slightly when he sits down next to me. At first he's angled away from me, his elbows on his knees but then he looks at me with a hurt in his eyes that makes me inch closer to him, and he does the same.

I may be angry about what he's done. What I've done as well. But no amount of anger can outweigh the pain we both feel in this moment.

The pain from knowing we're damaged beyond repair.

"Will you ever forgive me?" he questions and then takes a chance, moving his large hand to my thigh and gently rubbing his thumb back and forth.

"I already have," I tell him and feel slightly less strong. Weak for being okay with what's happened. Or at least for accepting it.

"Do you just not love me anymore then?" he asks me, his eyes piercing into mine and holding me captive. His words are raw, coming from a damaged man.

My lungs still and the words hang on the tip of my tongue. They're too afraid to leave me. I'm so weak for him, so bendable and disposable. If I admit such a flaw, he may never give me a fighting chance for something more.

What's worse, I may be content with that.

"Please just tell me you love me," Evan whispers. "I know I fuck up, more than I should. But please don't stop loving me."

"I've never felt so alone." It's one thing to be left alone. It's quite another to choose it. In this moment, I don't want it. I don't want to be alone another day, but I know I have to.

"I don't want to be alone. I don't want to be mad at you," I tell him, wiping from under my eyes and leaning my body into his. He kisses my forehead before enveloping me in his arms. And I let him. My biggest flaw.

"Then don't," he whispers and then pulls away to look down at me, waiting for my eyes to meet his. "Forgive me, please," he says and when I look to him, his dark hazel eyes beg me. His voice is raw and full of nothing but pain and remorse. "For everything. For being so stupid. For putting you through all this shit."

The question is right there, right on the tip of my tongue. I should ask, I should know what he's hiding. But the look in his eyes is so familiar.

"I meant what I said," I tell him. "I need you to leave."

"But you still love me?" he asks me even though it comes out as a statement.

My body heats, my breath stutters and the words get caught in my throat, refusing to come out. I'm on the edge of leaving him, of ruining this man I love so much.

"Yes, I still love you. So much," I admit and the confession is like a weight off my chest, but one that only leaves a gaping, painful hole in its absence.

"I can fix this."

"I need you to leave, Evan," I plead with him weakly.

"Just give me time."

"We're separated, Evan. That's what that means."

"I don't want this. Please, Kat." Evan closes his eyes and buries his face in the crook of my neck. I've never seen him so weak. So desperate for mercy.

I've never wanted to forgive so badly in my life, but it's not forgiveness that I need. It's a different life that I need moving forward and I won't get that with Evan.

"I'm sorry." My lips move but the words aren't audible, and I have to say it again.

His fingers dig into me, holding me closer and tighter, as if the moment he loosens them, I'll leave his grasp forever.

"I'm sorry, but it's what I want," I tell him and I've never heard such a horrible lie in my life. But he nods his head, pulling away slightly although still refusing to let go.

"It's what I deserve," he says beneath his breath. His eyes are glossy and his breathing slower as he looks away from me, still holding on but trying to gather the strength to say something. I don't trust myself to speak. So I just wait, praying for this moment to be over. Praying for something better to come once this has all left me. But how? I have no idea. I've never felt so dead inside.

"One last time. Please, just once more. I love you, Kat. I swear I've never loved anyone like I love you. And maybe it's not enough to keep you, but for tonight?"

Again I don't trust myself to speak. I'm not sure what words would pass through my lips. But I know what I want and I lean forward to take it, spearing my fingers through his hair and pressing my lips to his. It's only when I feel the wetness against our lips that I realize I was crying.

I let him hold me, and I try my best to remember every detail.

The way he smells, masculine like fresh pine and dew.

The way his heart beats just a bit faster than mine as I rest my palm against his hard chest.

I try to remember everything. I pray that I will, because even though he said he can make it right, I know he can't. I know that time will aid in the growing distance between us. I know we're leading two different lives.

I know I need more, and that I deserve someone who won't hide things from me and make me feel like I've lost myself.

So I need to remember this, because I want it to be the last time.

Not for him, not for us, but for me.

Chapter 24

Evan

Don't throw me away, don't tell me you're through.
Don't stop loving me, I can't live without you.
That ring on your finger, that makes you my wife.
You're my everything, my love and my life.

I didn't mean it when I said one last time. It's the same way an addict is desperate for more and will say anything to get it. All I have to do is be next to her when she needs a single thing. *Anything.* Just one small crack in her armor. At least that's what I keep hoping for.

It's what's keeping me from dissolving into the nothingness I feel in my hollow chest.

I wonder if she'll get over me before that time comes. If the few years we had together was enough to make her love me even when she doesn't want to. That's all I keep thinking about as I stare at her sleeping form. There's only a thin sheet over her gorgeous body, hiding it from me. Her back is toward me as she lies on her side, her hair fanned out along the pillow. I've been awake for hours; I'm not even sure I slept at all.

It feels like it's over, but that can't be true. I can't let her go this easily and walk away. But somehow it doesn't feel like letting her go. It feels like I don't have her anymore. Like I don't even have the option to keep her anymore.

A sudden buzz from my phone vibrating on the nightstand strips my thoughts from me and causes Kat to stir next to me.

I keep my eyes on her as I reach for it. She slowly turns to look over her shoulder and then looks away, pulling the sheet tighter around her. Closing herself off from me.

There's a heaviness on my chest as I let it sink in that she doesn't belong to me anymore. The bed dips as Kat pulls the sheet with her and walks quietly to the bathroom.

I would think my life couldn't get any lower than this, but the text from James mocks that thought.

My hands rake over my face as the phone drops and I inhale deeply, grateful Kat left when she did. There's still so much shit that I need to fix and make right. So much damage I've caused that's leaving cracks under each and every footstep I take.

Come to the office.

I stare at the text as Kat flicks on the light switch in the bathroom, the warm yellow hue filtering from under the closed door. She turns on the water as I toss the phone down.

James can go fuck himself.

It's like he knew I'd think that, because the second the phone drops to the nightstand, it goes off again.

It's not about work. You know what it's about.

I was given new information today.

The texts come one after the other in rapid speed and it makes adrenaline slowly pour into my veins, breathing life into me.

The creak of the bathroom door opening and the light switching off forces me to look up at Kat. She slipped on a robe in the bathroom. It's some sort of black and pink kimono from a bachelorette party I think. I've never seen her wear it but it's been hung up by the towels for years. I guess it's all she could find in there to hide herself from me.

She doesn't return my gaze and I can already see that she regrets last night.

Our last night.

I refuse to let it be true. I refuse to give up. But I'll give her time since that's what she thinks she needs.

"You can come whenever you need to," she says and then pulls a shirt over her head as she lets the robe fall into a puddle around her feet. The sight would make my dick hard as steel if it weren't for the words that hit me at full force. "To get whatever you need. I know you can't take everything all at once."

"You really want me to go?" I question even though I

know I need to leave regardless of what she tells me. I need time to sort out my shit and get my life to be one that belongs beside hers.

I wish she'd lie to me. I can see it in her eyes, her posture; I can hear it in her voice that she needs me to go. *Tell me a pretty lie, Kat. Make me believe you still want me.*

"I think it's for the best," she answers as her eyes flicker from me to the door and she pushes her hair out of her face. The dark circles under her eyes are evidence of how worn out she is. She's tired of my bullshit.

"I want to be happy and I feel like we're so used to being something else that it's not going to work."

The argument stirs in my chest, but she's right in a way and I know I can prove to her that we're going to be fine. I just need time. "I'll go now, but I'm coming back when I fix things."

"That's what you do, isn't it? You fix things?" A sarcastic, sad laugh accompanies her comment.

Fixer. That's what they call this job, but really I'm supposed to prevent anything from breaking. There's another small huff of a laugh that leaves her, but it's not the joyous sound I've grown to love so much. It's because of me. I'm the one who broke our marriage.

"I know we grew apart, but we're still together. Even if you want to pretend like we're not for a little while," I tell her. Climbing off the bed, I take a step to go to her, but she shakes her head slightly, crossing her arms and taking a step back.

"It was only one last time, Evan."

My mouth falls open just slightly for me to tell her last night wasn't the last time. I won't let it be. But the words don't come out. There's no conviction in that thought.

My eyes close as the phone in my hand buzzes again and I don't miss how Kat looks at it, a question in her eyes.

"It's James." I answer her unspoken question

She chews the inside of her cheek and doesn't acknowledge me in the least.

"I quit and I've just got to sign some paperwork." The lie slips out so easily. I'm almost ashamed at how easy it's become to hide the truth from her and disguise it as something normal and relatable.

I don't know if she can tell I'm lying, or if she just doesn't care anymore. She leaves me alone with nothing but a small nod in the bedroom we built together.

My blood turns cold and I stare at the open door. The pictures from the hall taunt me. I still hear the laughter. I remember the softness of her skin when they were taken.

The phone goes off again and it pisses me off.

I grit my teeth as I read the messages.

Get here in the next hour.

Out of spite, there's no fucking way I'll be at his office by then. I make sure to hit the message so he knows I read it. He can wait.

Chapter 25

Kat

It's supposed to hurt this much. I remind myself of that over and over again.

That's what a breakup is. It's pain. It's removing someone you once loved from your life. Erasing them as if they don't exist. As if they've died. And that's the most painful thing one can experience.

That's why it hurts so much. Because I'm supposed to be in agony.

"You look tired," I hear Jules say before she rests her hand on my shoulder, bringing me back into the moment. Standing in my small kitchen, with its clutter and a pile of dirty dishes in the sink, she's so out of place here. "Are you all right?" she asks me softly.

Before I can answer, the sounds of Maddie and Sue laughing over something drift into the room. The wine has been flowing, and half of the only remaining box of pizza is left on the counter. It's what I said I came in here for, another slice, but really I'd just remembered my time with Evan last night and then this morning and I wanted to be alone for a minute.

"You can tell me anything, Kat," Jules says in a voice drenched with empathy. I've always loved the person she is. But never more than now.

"I don't think I'm all right and I don't know if I ever will be," I answer and then arch my neck to stare at the ceiling, keeping my eyes open and trying not to bring this night down any more than I have.

"Is it normal to cry so much?" I ask her. "To be this emotional and this exhausted?"

"When you lose someone you love, yes." She answers easily and calmly, sending a wave of calm through my body, but even that makes me feel that much more exhausted.

"I wish I was past this stage."

"It'll happen before you know it. One day, the reminders won't hurt so badly. The mention of his name won't cut you to shreds. One day it'll feel like it's supposed to be this way."

"But I don't know if it is," I confess to her and then Sue ambles in from the dining room.

Her wineglass clinks on the counter as she sets it down

and then she catches a glimpse of me, her expression morphing to one of sympathy. An expression I learned to hate growing up, but right now, while I'm weak and feeling so lost, it's an expression that makes me lean into her when she opens her arms.

"You're all right, babe," she says softly and wraps her arms around me. Sue's arms are filled with warmth and she kisses my cheek too. "It's all right babe, we're here for you."

"Aww," I hear Maddie coo as she makes her way into the room.

"Let it all out," Sue says but I shake my head, my hair ruffling on her shoulder as I sniffle. Sue smells like wine. She sways a little and squeezes me tight. She's definitely more than tipsy.

"I'm sorry, guys. It wasn't supposed to turn into this." I push out the apology, wishing we were having the fun night I promised as I stand up straight and pull my shit together. Sue tries to hold on to me a little longer, but I push her away. I can handle this. At one point in my life I was so good at being alone.

"I'm fine," I tell them, stepping away for a moment and shaking out my hands. "I'm sorry."

It takes a few deep breaths and Sue refilling the empty glasses of wine on the counter for me to get over whatever this breakdown was.

"Don't be sorry. It's a sad time no matter how much you don't want it to be." Maddie's the first to say something and

Jules nods.

"It's going to be okay, though," Jules says and then Sue chimes in with, "You've got us, babe. We'll always be here for you, and that's all you need."

"Well, maybe a vibrator too," Sue adds a moment later and a genuine laugh erupts from my lips. It's short and unexpected, and fills the room. But it felt so good to laugh. To smile. To feel anything other than this darkness that's been a constant shadow over me.

"Do you want another?" Sue asks me, nearly spilling the wine from a glass poured too full as she tries to hand it to me. I haven't had a drink all night.

"If I do, I'm going to pass out." Just as I answer, another yawn hits me. "It's been a while since I've been able to sleep through the night."

"I'll take it," Maddie offers and immediately sets it back down on the counter.

"So it's really over?" Sue asks and then takes a sip. For the first time, I see something in her eyes I haven't before. I see sorrow. Genuine pain. As if even Sue was rooting for us. Sue, the valiant heroine against men who cheat and lie.

I nod, ignoring how the emotions swell up again. I haven't told them that he cheated on me back when we first started dating. I can't admit it. I don't want to say the words out loud and make them real. I don't want them to see him as a villain. I love him too much to paint him in that light. Or maybe it's the shame that I still love him even after knowing what he did.

"We're just in two different places and it's better to be apart." I shrug and add, "But we always were, you know? Like this shouldn't be too shocking."

"He doesn't want to change?" Maddie asks. There's always hope in Maddie and I wish I could hold on to that.

"Men don't change," Sue says woefully. "I'm sorry. I'm doing it again," she says, shaking her head. "Sometimes it still hurts, you know? And I don't want you to go through what I did. I promise you, it's the last thing I want for you." Her voice gets a little tight, but she shakes it off quickly.

I love Sue, and I remember how hard her divorce was on her. But I swear this is different. *It has to be.* Her ex was vile and brutal. Evan isn't any of that. He'd never hurt me intentionally. He's just ... he's just Evan.

"He said he wants to fix it," I answer as I watch Maddie sip from the glass without picking it up. Instead she crouches down, bringing her lips to the rim to sip. My lips tug into an asymmetrical smile for just a moment at the sight.

"It's not what he says." The hardness in her voice is absent, but there's still a finality in Sue's statement. "It would be hard for him to change, wouldn't it? He's been this way for years."

It's meant to be a rhetorical question, but the answer rings clear in my head. He did something bad. Something that he needed an alibi for. That's enough of a reason to change everything at once.

I stare at the dark red liquid. Sue's voice turns to white noise as she tells a story about something that makes the other girls laugh and I laugh too, when they do. I don't know if it's the first time he's needed an alibi. Or the second or the third. But it's the first time he changed. I knew something was off before the article. Before he told me anything. Before the lies.

I knew something was different.

And I didn't even bother to ask him what he'd done.

Chapter 26

Evan

There's a slow prick of irritation crawling down my spine as I sit in the chair across from James. Every limb feels the need to move, like a spider is climbing its way down my back. My fingers dig into the hard wood of the armrests as I stay perfectly still, staring down my former boss. Former friend. Now enemy.

"You aren't the best at listening," he says from across the room as he closes a drawer. The city lights creep in through the window behind him, casting shadows over the large desk.

"I don't follow orders," I grit out from between clenched teeth. My words come out menacing, but I don't mean for them to. One more meeting, and this is over. I'm done with him. He's yet to get that message or to tell me what the hell is going on.

James leans forward, clasping his hands together and his perfectly tailored suit wrinkles beneath his arms, making the fabric look cheap. He's always looked just a bit cheap. Regardless of the brand or how expensive his tastes are. Some assholes will always look like a knockoff.

He taps his fingers on the desk, but my eyes don't leave his. "The reason I called you in here is simple, Evan. The new client we have likes to live on the reckless side, and I'm concerned about drug abuse."

A gruff exhale leaves me from deep down in my chest. "I quit." I ignore the fact that he's hinting around what happened with Tony. My skin tingles and that feeling of a spider crawling on me comes back. I can't help but think he's recording this conversation. Everything in my gut has been telling me there's a setup and that I'm going to take the fall for what happened.

It was my fault, so I should be taking the blame regardless. On my terms, not this prick's and he's responsible for the way it went down. Some of the blame rests on his shoulders.

"I know what you said, but I assumed you'd come to your senses," he says, waving off my curt response. "Like I said, the new client has been known to behave a bit recklessly and I just want to make sure the policy we had in place remains the same."

The policy. I smirk at him, my grip on the arms getting

tighter although my fingers are all that move.

The policy where the clients get what they want, but we don't say it out loud to anyone. The one where we're given clean stashes of the best drugs in the rec rooms. That's the policy. Instead of clarifying the policy, I answer, "After what happened with Tony I would think it's more than clear that we should advise our clients against anything too reckless."

James's eyes narrow. He knows I know that he's recording this. I'm not a fool. The only question I have is why. Why record it? More blackmail? Or evidence? What's he after?

I stare him in the eyes as I ask, "What is it you really want? You know you've provided drugs to clients before." I cock my head to the side as I ask, "Are we changing the policy?"

"I've never given anyone anything illegal," he states and I notice how he stiffens slightly but still tries to act casual as he shrugs and adds, "There's no change to the policy."

My wife has this thing she does. It's a smile I hate. A smirk really. I hate it when she gives it to me. It's one that tells me she knows I'm full of shit. While I sit here, staring at this asshole, I can feel the corner of my lips tug up into that sarcastic smirk. It doesn't stay there for long, though.

"Did you know the coke was laced?" James asks me and it takes a moment for the question to register.

The coke I gave Tony.

That doesn't make sense. Our shit is clean and pure and the best there is.

It's also provided to us in the recreation room by the company.

"I wouldn't know a thing about that." It's the only answer I can force out. Keeping a hard stare on my face even as my blood heats hotter and hotter.

Is he serious? It was laced?

I know the laws in and out. I can't admit to any knowledge that could lead back to me. I can accuse him, but not admit to participation or any foresight of drugs being gifted so freely when asked.

I raise my hand as if I'm the one in the wrong. The one who misspoke. "None of it matters anyway. I told you, I quit."

"And I told you, that you—"

"I'm done," I say and my words come out hard as I stand up and tower over the desk. James is quick to get up, tugging at one sleeve and then the other on his suit. "I thought you had something to tell me. Something useful and not some delusion that you could use to blackmail me."

His eyes glint with a darkness at my words. "It's not blackmail. I haven't—"

"Fuck you, James," I say, cutting him off as I turn my back to him to stalk out of the room. It'll be the last time I come here.

"You know what I can do to you," James says the threat to my back.

"I'm calling your bluff," I respond out of anger and instantly regret it, but I don't stop. All the weeks of not knowing if him or Samantha would tell the cops what happened, all the guilt and denial rise up in my chest and cause the next words come out without my consent. "Tell them what happened."

Just the thought of the truth getting out lifts a weight off of me.

"Tell them I gave him the coke. Tell them I set him up to get high and came back to him dead. Tell the press. Tell everyone," I say and my heart beats faster and faster as my hands ball into white-knuckled fists. I realize what I've just done. I realize I've said it out loud. But I don't care. It doesn't change anything. None of it matters anymore.

"It's murder, Evan, and you know it," James says as I face the door to leave. Not bothering to acknowledge him in the least.

Yes, it's murder. And it's not the first time something's happened under my watch. But it's the last. I'm done with this shit and this life.

I didn't lace a damn thing. If that stash was messed with, it wasn't me and I'm not going down for a crime I didn't commit. I'll own up to everything else.

I want to pay for my sins and chase what truly matters to me.

A love I took for granted. A love I don't know if I can salvage.

Chapter 27

Kat

Pulled in every direction,
Too dizzy to stay still.
My feet stumble beneath me,
My body frozen from the chill.
No more of being numb and weak,
No more of waiting, left in vain.
I've had enough of lies,
I've had enough of pain.

The buzz from the townhouse speaker rouses me from my seat in the dining room. *Buzz. Buzz.* It's an annoying high-pitched sound that I can't stand.

My head's already throbbing. It's been like this for hours, ever since I got home and took the test. I can't go back and look at it. It's hard enough to wrap my head around everything that's happening.

And the guilt ...

As I walk to the front of the townhouse, hustling down the stairs so I don't have to hear that damn noise again, I realize it's nearly nine and I'm still in my pajamas. At least I have pants on, but the matching light gray cotton shirt has a large spot of coffee on the front and I'm sure my hair's a mess.

"Who is it?" I ask in a voice that sounds more together than I feel as I push the button down and then release it. The only person I can think of is Henry, Evan's father.

"Sorry to bother you, I was just hoping for a quick meeting," a voice says on the other side and it takes me a moment to recognize it.

"Jacob?" I say into the intercom.

"I hope you don't mind. I was in the area and wanted to stop by," he replies and his voice breaks up over the speaker.

I know it's rude to make him wait, it's unkind not to answer him immediately, but this is so unexpected. I don't know how to react or respond.

"I'm not quite dressed for company," I tell him and then close my eyes from embarrassment. He still hasn't signed with the agency and I haven't spoken to him since running into him on the street.

"That's all right with me," he answers easily and I lean into the button, keeping it held down as my head throbs again and my eyes close with frustration.

"Is it all right if I come up?"

"Of course," I answer out of instinct. "Come on up," I tell him and then hit the buzzer to let him up. My heart races as I consider why he's here. I know why, deep down. It's my fault. I led him on.

A sarcastic laugh leaves me as I throw my head back and wipe my tired eyes with my hands. How self-centered and presumptuous I am to think he's here for anything other than business. I ignore the guilt and the worry that riddle my body and glance in the large oval mirror in the foyer as I wait for Jacob to make his way up the stairs.

There are bags under my eyes and a smattering of eyeliner from yesterday still remaining. I wipe carefully under them and pull my hair back, but I still don't look professional. My simple black leggings and a baggy shirt are made somewhat better by slipping on a crocheted sweater. It's better than nothing, laid back at the very best. I find it hard to care that much about my appearance as I open the front door.

I'm caught off guard as he walks up the stairs and comes into view. Of course I look like hell when he looks charming in a relaxed kind of way. His hair is ruffled, but probably gelled to look like it's slightly messy. It's his stubble, though, that gets me. I have a type, and Jacob fits that type to a T. Maybe that's how I know this is going to be trouble.

He gives me a wide smile and doesn't seem to care about

my appearance in the least.

"I was just going to call it an early night," I lie, trying to stand with dignity in front of Jacob.

"Oh shit, I'm sorry, Kat." It's odd hearing him call me Kat. Most of my clients don't use my nickname. It's too casual. A type of casual I usually put an end to immediately, but I can't bring myself to correct him.

"What are you doing here, Jacob?" I ask warily. We don't have an appointment, and quite frankly I'm not in a state to be professional.

"It's Jake, remember?" he answers playfully and God help me, but I blush. "I was wondering if I could maybe take you out for coffee? I was hoping for dinner. If not tonight, then ..."

"I'm sorry, I don't think that's something," I stammer over my words. "Jacob ..." I clear my throat and continue, "Jake, I hope I didn't give you the wrong impression." I suck in a breath and push the stray hairs out of my face.

"It's nothing at all that you did, I just," he pauses to take a deep breath and smiles before letting out a small laugh. "It was stupid of me. I'm sorry, Kat. I just thought maybe there was a little attraction on your side?" he asks although it's a statement.

"Jake, I'm ..." I want to say married, taken, in love with another man. The last line would be true. I'll always love Evan, and nothing will ever change that.

"I thought maybe you would like some company," he states, tilting his head as he leans against the wall. The muscles on his shoulders ripple as he does it. "I went through something a bit ago and I know I could use a distraction."

A distraction would be nice. I can't help that the thought makes me more relaxed each second that passes.

His half smile and gentle sigh are what do me in as he shrugs and slips his hands into his pockets. "I thought maybe you needed someone. Or that you'd like the company." He's even more handsome when he looks at me like that. It's a look that makes me feel warmth running through me. Compassion and understanding.

I've never been so tempted in my life. I so desperately need someone. I need someone to pick me up and force me to think about something else, because I'm a hopeless wreck.

"It's very sweet of you and I won't lie," I start to say and then hesitate to finish the thought, but settle on the basic truth. "I wouldn't act on anything because I just can't right now. I would never forgive myself and it wouldn't be fair to you." My words are rushed at the end, trying to defend my decision and assuage me of the guilt I'm feeling.

"Hey," Jacob says with an easy tone that breaks through the anxiety washing over me. His reassuring voice forces me to look into his gentle gaze. It's comforting and relaxing and makes me not trust myself. "How about this? How about you call me if you think you want to hang out or talk, or whatever it is that's on your mind?" he asks in a soothing tone that's almost melodic. It calms me, each word a consoling balm to the hurt that rages through my body.

I want that. More than anything, I want this pain that I feel to stop. I would give anything to make it go away. Jacob could do that, but it would be short-lived. I blink away the haze of lust, the cloud of want and desire leaving me slowly, very slowly. I clear my throat and look him in the eyes as I tell him, "I can't."

"'Cause we're going to work together?" he asks, although the way he tilts his head and strains his words makes it more than obvious that he knows why I can't. My lips form a thin straight line as I shake my head no.

"You love him?"

"I do, but that's not why. I'm just—I'm not okay and I need to figure things out ..." I can't finish the thought, but thankfully I don't have to.

"I understand," Jacob says and runs his hand through his thick hair. My eyes are caught in his as I nod in thanks.

"Let's pretend this didn't happen then?"

"I'd rather you remember," he says with a grin that makes me crave him more. "I'll be here when you're ready," he says and then turns to leave. To walk away from me and leave me alone in my misery, just as I asked.

For a second I want to reach out and stop him from leaving; I don't want to go back to what's waiting for me. I don't want to face what I have to do.

But my fingers grip the edge of the foyer doorway as Jacob

turns away and heads to the front door.

"I'll talk to you later then?"

I should say no. I should cut off whatever this is. It's dangerous and I can feel myself heading toward an edge where I won't be able to balance. I can see myself falling. And that's why I give him a small smile and nod my head. "Later," I say, the word slipping from my lips like a sin.

Chapter 28

Evan

The radio in the car is silenced as I turn off the ignition. It's not often I get a parking spot so close to the townhouse. It was a sacrifice we made when we bought the place a few years ago.

My head falls back against the leather headrest and I stare up at the building, at the top two floors on the right side, knowing that Kat's in there. So close, but so damn far away just the same.

My phone pings just as I open the door to get out and drag my sorry ass up to tell her everything. To lay it all out there, beg for her forgiveness, her understanding. But most importantly for her to stay with me. I'll give her space and time. I'll give her everything she asks. All I need is a deadline or something to work toward. I need her.

If she can still love me, after all I put her through and everything ahead of us, then we can get through anything.

I expect it to be Kat who messaged, but it's not her that texted me. It's Samantha.

I heard you quit.

News travels fast, I respond quickly and then debate on how to tell her I won't be responding anymore to her. It's not fair to my wife and now that I've left the company, there's no reason to have any type of relationship with her.

What about what happened?

I stare at the text on my phone as the lights in my car dim, signaling me to leave. She follows up the question with another that makes my stomach churn. *He knows about what happened and you know he won't let it go. He'll hang this over your head until he gets what he wants.*

My brow knits as I read the message. I don't give a shit what he knows or what he wants. For a moment, I think maybe she's messaging the wrong person. I settle on my response.

I have nothing to give him.

He knows about us, Evan.

I stare at the text message, letting it sink in.

You told him? I ask her, my gaze shifting from the phone to the lit townhouse building off the busy city street. The lights are on in her office and the living room. So close. She's so close.

My phone vibrates in my hand and I look back down to see her response. *He's known for years.*

My hand clenches tight as I realize he's been playing me. He's never let on that he knew I fucked his wife.

My first instinct is to blame Sam. *You didn't tell me you told him*, I text and then hate myself for it. I didn't know she was married; we were both high and I wanted any excuse to end things with Kat.

I didn't think he cared.

It was years ago. So now what? I swallow the ball of heat rising in my throat. It doesn't change anything. If he wants to be pissed, he can be pissed.

I don't see him letting this go. Not when he can get back at you. You need to be careful.

A frustrated groan travels up my throat.

Fuck him. He can do what he wants, but I'm not his bitch.

My phone immediately vibrates as I slip it into my pocket, and I cuss as I take it back out. Not to read her response, only to shut it off, silencing it and ignoring all the problems that wait for me. I'm done with both of them. I'm done with it all.

I swallow thickly and step out into the cool night, the city traffic surrounding me as I shut the car door and leave it all behind.

Everything is crumbling around me, but the only thing I care about is losing Kat. I don't see how I can hold on to her when I don't have a plan and I've lost control.

She needs a better man, and I swear I can be one. We'll start over and do it right this time.

I run my hand down my face. Hitting the lock, the car beeps and the bright headlights flash in the dark of the night. The sounds of the city streets are loud as I walk up the sidewalk, past men and women who carry on with their busy lives and don't have a clue how mine is being ripped apart.

I'll confess and then pack a box, and let her know it's only a separation and that even after I'll still love her and want her. That I'll do anything. I'll keep coming back, fighting for her. I'm not saying goodbye, I'm only doing what she asks because I love her and I know she needs time.

The keys jingle in my hand as I make my way home. Every second I'm trying to think of the best way to come clean about everything to Kat. She deserves to know, even if she hates me once she finds out. I have to tell her first.

A heavy breath leaves me as I turn the lock and walk into the building, running a hand over my hair and trying to block the image of her disappointment from my mind.

I can imagine how her deep green eyes will widen, how her lips will part and how she'll think I'm lying at first. I already know how she'll look at me, how she'll question who I am and why or if, she loves me.

My footsteps are heavy as I grip the iron railing and head to the top of the stairwell, to our home we've built together, the one she's kicked me out of. My gut feels heavy, churning with a sickness that rises to my chest as I hear her voice and recall the memory of her telling me to get out. My fingers wrap tighter around the rail, keeping me upright as I force myself to continue. I need to confess and come clean.

I want Kat back and the life we once had. It's all I need to live.

Every thought is lost at the sight in front of me. My blood turns ice cold when I stop at the top of the stairs where Kat's talking to that asshole from the café. Her voice is kind and nurturing and the way she offers him a sad smile ... fuck no.

My legs feel like they're trembling; my body's shaking from the sight of him. Jacob, the supposed client Kat said was no one. *No one.* Yet he stands only feet away from the front door.

Anger rises quickly as I watch them. I knew there was something between them. I could tell. I know my wife and I know men like this prick.

"You motherfucker," I sneer the words without thinking twice. The door to my townhouse is still cracked when this dumb fuck looks up at me.

"What are you doing?" Kat calls out with shock as she stands in the doorway.

Chapter 29

Kat

I'd recognize Evan's voice anywhere, but the anger is terrifyingly new. The second I grip the cold handle and open the door, my body freezes and the shock makes my mouth hang open and my eyes go wide. My heart beats in what feels like slow motion.

"Stop it!" I scream at him. My words echo in my head as he slams his fist against Jacob's jaw. It's instantly red and swollen and Evan's already got his other fist up.

Holy shit!

"Evan!" I scream as I run out of the foyer and into the hallway. "Stop it!" I yell and grip onto his arm. I slam both of my hands into Evan's chest, managing to separate the two men as Jacob grabs his jaw.

"You fucked my wife," Evan yells over me, screaming at Jacob and this time I want to smack Evan straight across his face. I don't. I don't give him any reaction except to turn toward Jacob to apologize.

"I'm so sorry," I offer Jacob who keeps a surprised smile on his face, as if it didn't bother him in the least.

"You fucked—"

"Stop it!" I scream again, and this time my voice feels raw and it pains me to scream. My body's hot and shaking, adrenaline coursing through my blood as my heart races.

"Get out of here," I say as I usher Jacob away. His green eyes flash with something, perhaps disbelief.

"You're cheating on me," Evan says it as if it's a question, his nostrils flaring and his hands still clenched into fists.

"You're an idiot," I say, keeping my voice low, apologizing again to Jacob and feeling the heat of embarrassment.

"It was a sucker punch," Jake says loud enough for Evan to hear. "And no, I didn't sleep with Kat." He looks Evan dead in the eye with the last line.

Embarrassment and horror wrap themselves tight around me as Jake leaves.

With my throat tight and arms crossed, I face Evan and say, "I'm not the one keeping secrets, you fucking asshole. He's a client and nothing more." My gaze almost shifts away from him. I know there was something, a chemistry that kindled between Jacob and me. A tension that I wanted to push. But it's only because I was hurting, and I never submitted to the temptation. I couldn't hurt Evan like that. I never would.

"What is wrong with you?" My question is dripping with nothing but disdain. For a moment I think of all the questions on the tip of my tongue, asking him why he's doing it and when he turned into this man. But this is the man I married. I'm the one who's changed. Not him.

Evan takes a step forward and his hand raises to my shoulder. I smack him away, barely feeling his hot skin against mine. "Don't touch me," I yell at him. My hand stings from the impact and I can't stand it.

I can't stand what we've become.

Evan's shoulders rise and fall steadily.

"Kat," he says and his voice cracks, like my name strangles him as he whispers it again. He takes a hesitant step forward, raising his arms and the blood from his torn knuckles is all I can see.

"What were you thinking?" I can barely ask him. Evan's expression falls and he looks past me. It's only then that I turn and see that Jake is gone. "What's wrong with you?"

"What was he doing here?"

"I've never cheated on you, and I wouldn't. Ever. Evan, I can't deal with this. The partying and what you're doing. Punching people for no damn good reason!"

"I quit, Kat. And you sure as hell know what it looked like.

If he didn't fuck you, he wanted to."

"What the hell are you doing here?"

"I came to tell you everything," he says and his admission changes the tension in an instant. The evening is seemingly colder in the blink of an eye.

"I might ... I might have some things happen." He closes his eyes and moves his hands to his hair. Hands with split knuckles and traces of blood.

Was he always like this? I want to hold and comfort him. But it's no use.

"I was stupid."

"Evan, you've had years to be stupid. Years of me begging you to grow up." Every word hurts more and more. I know I'm not going to give him what he needs. I can't anymore.

"I wanted you to be my partner." I whisper the words, my voice laced with disappointment.

"I thought that's what we were."

"I need someone who's ready for the next stage of life." I barely get the words out as my throat dries and closes, threatening to suffocate me. But I finish the thought, making my heart split into two as I look deep into Evan's eyes and tell him, "Or no one at all."

"Kat," Evan says, whispering my name as if it's a threat. One against him. Or maybe it's a plea. "I'm sorry, okay?"

My head shakes and the words won't come out.

"I'm sorry I hit him, it looked bad at first. It looked like something else to me, but even then I shouldn't have hit him."

"No, you shouldn't have."

"It was shitty of me. I'm sorry. I'm so sorry," he says and I believe him. But it's not enough. He's still the same Evan.

I wipe the tears from my eyes with the back of my hand as I shake my head. "I can't do this anymore." It's the truth and even though it's the worst pain that I've felt in my entire life, I know it needs to be done. "I will be better on my own."

"Don't say that," Evan pleads, but he stands there not moving, his hands by his sides and his body stiff with disbelief. Or maybe fear. "I can't lose you," he says. I feel like my heart is breaking, but I shake my head.

"Maybe I should just be alone." My eyes burn with more tears as I shake my head again and say, "No, I need to. I need to be alone. I'm sorry," my voice fails me as I whisper the apology. I hate hurting him; I can't stand the pain in his eyes and expression. He doesn't try to hide it in the least, and it shreds me.

But we're just not meant for each other, not with the lives we're leading.

"I love you."

"Love isn't enough!" I yell and hate myself. I truly do. "It's not enough anymore," I say, steadying my voice although it's still low. I cross my arms and try to keep myself together, I try to hold my body upright although it begs me to collapse.

"Is that what you want?"

"I want a divorce," I say the lie in a single breath. The

words all come out at once, bunched together and needing to be said, to be heard. To be felt to the very core of who Evan is.

My fingertips dig into my forearms as I slowly raise my eyes to his and the conviction wavers.

He doesn't speak, although his lips part once and then again. He licks them as his brow furrows and he visibly swallows then looks past me at the empty wall. Again he starts to say something but stops, clasping and unclasping his hands and trying to find some way to tell me what he's thinking.

The worst part is that I want him to say something. I need him to give me something to hold on to him.

I'd go mad waiting to hear him tell me he'll make this right. For him I'd fall again, I know I would. There isn't enough strength in my body to keep me from Evan.

But he doesn't say a word; he never does when I need him to.

It takes a long moment. Each second my heart beats, the steady sound is all I can hear. And then he turns his back to me and walks away without saying another word.

My body is freezing as I slowly turn from the hall and head toward our door. I can't breathe, but somehow I am. I can't manage a thought, but my mind is whirling with the image of what just happened.

The way he spoke my name like he needed me. The way his voice was laced with desperation and his eyes shined with determination, but then failure. The way his expression crumbled when he realized he lost me.

I don't stop walking until I get back to our bedroom, barely glancing at the unmade bed and remembering the last time we shared it and everything about that night. I can still feel his lips on my neck, his hands traveling ever so slowly down my body as he whispered how much he loves me. And I believe the sentiment. No one has ever loved me like Evan, and no one else ever will.

It's just not enough.

For me, I'd go back to him. I'd let him do what he wanted and I'd pay the price. I head into the bathroom.

I pick up the small plastic stick still hanging off the edge of the sink.

My head's been a mess the past month. I didn't realize I'd missed one period, let alone two.

It's the brightest set of pink lines. I may not be the best friend I can be, or the best wife for that matter. But for my child, I'll be the best mother I can be and that starts with saying no to the life I once lived and had with Evan.

My hand splays on my lower belly as I lean my back against the edge of the sink. I have to tell him and I will, but not yet. I need to stop loving him first. I need to move on and focus on what I can change and make better for what's to come.

It's not just me who deserves that anymore.

Chapter 30

Evan

I promise to love you forever. And that's the easy part.

To honor and cherish you.

To keep your wishes and dreams my own.

To comfort you and keep you safe, always.

Till death do us part.

My wedding vows haunt me. The parts of them I can remember, at least. I can't stop seeing the look of complete devotion on Kat's face on our wedding day, as I read my vows from the scrap of paper where I'd written them.

My heart raced as I spoke each word, my gaze straying from the paper to look back at her. She was so beautiful, with a love that I knew I didn't deserve.

I can still remember the feel of her soft skin as I cupped her cheek in my hand. I can still smell the sweet fragrance that drifted toward me as I leaned closer to her, all of our friends and family clapping and cheering as I took my first kiss from my wife.

I can still taste her lips on mine.

When I said those words, I meant them. I thought they'd be so easy to keep, to be honest, and it never occurred to me that I'd forget.

A large metal door opens at the end of the hall and I look up, my view obstructed by steel bars of the jail cell.

It's been a long damn time since I've been locked up. Years. Almost a dozen years, to be exact. I knew I'd be back soon, though.

It was only a matter of time before they brought me in for questioning. Samantha tried to warn me but it was too late. Soon after I left the townhouse the cops picked me up and brought me in. I sit hunched over, resting my forearms on my thighs as I wait for the attending officer to come get me. With the footsteps echoing down the small corridor, my gaze raises in anticipation, only to drop again to the cement floor. He walks right past me without a glance in my direction and I drop my head, focusing on the cracks in the concrete and recalling every detail of the night that put me here.

My hands sweat as I twist my wedding band around my finger. I can't think about Kat right now or what she'd say.

I haven't told her a damn thing about this and we're in the same place we were when I last left.

The worst part about all of this is that I don't have a way out yet. I'm falling into a dark hole, not knowing how I can escape, or if it will ever end. Never in my life has a situation seemed so dire and I'm more than aware that I miss her presence the most. It would make all this hell seem insignificant if only I knew she still loved me.

Someone coughs and I slowly turn my head to the left where it came from a few cells down, but I can't see a damn thing but bars and concrete. I think there's only one other person in holding with me. And he's on the same side so the rest of the cells are empty. I guess Tuesdays are slow days for the station.

My foot tap, tap, taps on the ground as I wait. The cops haven't given me any information to go on yet. Other than the word *murder*. My best guess is that they think I gave Tony the coke and knew it was laced with something deadly.

Even if I didn't know it was tainted, I'd still be held accountable. At least here in the state of New York, I am. If it was deliberately tampered with, though ... then someone *wanted* him dead. Although the only two people who knew it was even there were me and James.

My shoulders rise with a heavy breath as the anger gets the best of me. Rage seeps into my blood just thinking his name. The image of him flickers in front of me the second I close my eyes. He smiled as he patted my back, walking out of the room after making sure it'd be ready for our client, Tony.

He's the one who put it there. The only question I have on my mind is whether he's the one who laced it. I can't imagine he did. He wouldn't be that stupid, but I'm not taking the fall for murder. Not to save his skeevy ass. I'm not a rat, but if James plays his cards against me—the proof that I was with Tony before he died, then I'm taking that fucker down.

"Thompson," the cop's voice bellows and echoes off the walls of the small cell.

"That's me," I answer, looking the detective square in his light blue eyes. I don't recognize him as he puts the key in the lock and opens the door wide for me to get out and walk to the interrogation room. Adrenaline pumps hard in my blood. It seems more intense now than it did years ago.

Maybe it's because I don't know how I'll get out of this. I have an alibi, but if James showed them the pictures proving I was with Tony that night, then I'm fucked.

I have to wonder if he would, though. If that's the case, he was deliberately withholding evidence and they'd have to question his intentions and his involvement, as well as the fact that he lied during the first questioning. He could do it anonymously, though, and knowing his character, he'd sure as hell take that route.

My boots smack against the floor and I walk at an easy pace, making sure I don't do anything to piss off the cop. He's a short guy. Probably in his thirties, I guess. Lots of wrinkles around his eyes, though. Maybe from the stress of the job, maybe from the sun.

"After you," he says with a grim look pulling his lips into a thin line as he opens the door. I give him a nod and walk in; he doesn't follow.

I only hesitate to sit down for a moment. There are two men in the room already. A tall cop with broad shoulders and a thin mustache that I want to shave off and Jay McCann, the lawyer from James's PR firm.

"You're fired," I tell Jay the second I sit down. I don't even look at the slick lawyer. He's represented me and plenty of other clients before, but I know he'd break attorney-client privilege and tell James everything. I don't trust him.

"Are you sure?" the cop questions, not hiding his surprise in the least and glancing between the two of us as McCann stumbles over a response. Jay is obviously shocked and I don't blame him.

"Evan," Jay starts, his voice strong although he instinctively reaches to loosen the knot of the dark navy tie that matches his suit, "I highly suggest we talk about this before you—"

"Yes, I'm sure. Sorry, Jay." I turn to face him and wait for a response, but he stands up and straightens his jacket. His clean-shaven jaw clenches as he grabs his briefcase and I can see he wants to say something, but he holds it in.

Probably a good call on his part.

I watch him walk around the table and exit without another word, leaving me alone with the cop.

"I'm Detective Bradshaw, Mr. Thompson."

"I would say it's nice to meet you, but ..." I reply with a smirk and tilt my hands out with my palms up. Detective Bradshaw doesn't laugh or respond to my little joke and that's fine. They never do in here where it's recorded. I know how this works.

"Have you been informed of your rights?"

"I have," I answer him.

"And do you know what you're being charged with?"

"Charged?" I say and although I keep my voice even, my back stiffens slightly as my muscles tense. "I wasn't informed I was being charged with anything." That statement comes out far too casually for the adrenaline racing through me.

"Well, I imagine there's no refuting the charge on your part. You supplied Tony Lewis with the cocaine he overdosed on."

"You want me to admit to handing over the cocaine to him, so you have someone behind bars to take the fall for a hotshot's death?" I ask him sarcastically, seamlessly hiding how my nerves want to crack and how my blood pounds in my ears. I let out an uneasy huff of a laugh and shake my head. Leaning back in my seat, I look him in the eyes with a smile as I say, "That's not happening, Detective."

"Well, someone is going to go down for murder, yes." He sucks his teeth as he stands up and crosses his arms over his chest. "You'd only be sentenced for your part and we're willing to cut you a deal. Whoever laced it with fentanyl intended for it to kill. There's no doubt in the DA's mind that it's murder, Mr. Thompson. I'd take the deal if I were you."

He waits for a reaction, but I use every ounce of energy in me to not give him anything. I won't say a word. Inside, I'm denying it. No fucking way. There's no way James would give a client something that would kill him. They're wrong. If it wasn't James ... then who?

"We know it's someone within the firm. It's not the first time one of New York Stride Public Relation's clients have turned up dead." He leans back and adds, "As I'm sure you're aware."

As he talks, he half pushes, half tosses the manila folder that was sitting on his end of the table my way. It lands with a heavy thud in front of me and I open it, feigning disinterest.

"Nothing points to that person being you, but this was intentional. Someone wanted whoever was going to be taking this coke to die. It was laced with enough fentanyl to kill instantly."

I don't say anything as he pauses, opening the manila folder when I don't and pulling out a page with charts and shit I don't know anything about. He points his finger to a graph, then taps it far too hard, turning his knuckles white. "Whoever did it wanted even the smallest dose to kill."

Silence. All I do is stare at the man and then force my gaze back down, to the photos of Tony, dead on the floor of that hotel room.

"If you have any information on how we'd go about finding the killer, that'd be useful, and we'd certainly be grateful for that."

I have to calmly exhale a few times, keeping as still as possible and making sure my expression doesn't change in the least before I can respond. "I really liked Tony and it's a shame what happened to him. It's extremely upsetting to think someone murdered him."

"It is, especially since he didn't have any enemies we can find," the cop answers, his voice tighter now and then he leans forward.

"You know, if we can't find who did it, you'll be taking the full brunt of things."

I let a sarcastic laugh rock my shoulders and then look toward the door to my left. The one that leads to my freedom. "I'm sorry, Detective, everyone I know loved Tony and I didn't give him any drugs." I lean forward, mimicking his posture as I add, "It's illegal."

"If that's the way you want to play it." His jaw is tense as he reaches for the folder and I lean back in my seat again and only watch as he collects the papers.

"Am I free to go now? I'd like to leave."

He stands up abruptly, pushing the chair back a few inches, making the steel chair legs scrape noisily across the floor. "I don't think so. Maybe a night in the cells will help you remember something."

Fucking prick. Not that I'm surprised. It's a game of chess and his side has more pieces and a head start. I stay still and wait, keeping my guard up.

"Be back in a bit, Thompson."

I clench my jaw and crack my knuckles as I watch him leave.

It's only when the door shuts and I'm left alone in the room that I realize the extent of what Detective Bradshaw said.

Someone *wanted* to kill Tony, knowing I'd give the coke to him. Maybe even thinking I'd take it too. I'm known for partying. It's why clients choose me to represent them in the firm. My head spins as I try to recall that night. I don't broadcast that I'm not a cokehead and a glass of whiskey is enough for me. Still, everyone in the scene knows I'm down for whatever they're in the mood for. There's no way anyone else could have gotten in there. James had the master key, and he gave me the only other copy.

I was there to party with the clients and make sure they had a good time, but stayed out of trouble. It was easy enough in the rec room.

For the last ten minutes, I've been thinking that someone was trying to kill Tony. It's what the detective was suggesting.

I'd bet anything that James thought I'd take a hit at least.

Maybe it's paranoia, but as I sit alone in the room, all I can think is that the coke was never intended for Tony.

Someone wanted me dead.

This is not the end of Kat and Evan's story.
Their duet continues with

You Know I Need You.

About the Author

Thank you so much for reading my romances. I'm just a stay at home Mom and an avid reader turned Author and I couldn't be happier.

I hope you love my books as much as I do!

More by Willow Winters
www.willowwinterswrites.com/books

Printed in Great Britain
by Amazon